SOUTHERN SPELLS

SWEET TEA WITCHES BOOK TWO

AMY BOYLES

ONE

"*B*e still, dagnabit," my grandmother said to a box that rattled and shook as if alive.

"Um, what's in there?" I said, pointing at the cardboard.

It looked completely ordinary, right down to the UPS label on the side. But the fact that the thing quivered like it contained a chest-ripping alien lifeform had me worried.

And the fact was, I wouldn't put it past my grandmother, Betty Craple, to have such a thing in a box.

"Don't tell anyone," she said. We were in the sunny yellow kitchen of her house. She set the box on the table and grabbed a knife from the butcher block. "It just came in today. I've been waiting forever for this beauty."

"It's not going to kill me, is it?" I said.

"No, but I wouldn't look at it cross-eyed. They tend to get mad when you do that," she said.

"What does?" my cousin Amelia said, sailing into the room. She had short blond hair and delicate pixie features. She grabbed the carafe of hot coffee and poured herself a steaming cup. "Want one?" she said to me.

"Yes." I yawned and rubbed the sleep from my eyes. I took the cup she poured and deciding that it needed some jazzing up, I fisted a handful of jelly beans from a dish and plopped them in.

"You might be making unicorn coffee, but it won't make you poop rainbows," Betty said.

"It's unicorn hot chocolate, not coffee," I said, blowing in my cup. "And I like jelly beans for breakfast. Now, what sort of monster are you hiding in that box?"

Betty's eyes gleamed with pride. "For years I've been trying to be Melbalean Mayes at Cotton and Cobwebs."

"Melba toast who?" I said.

"Melba-lean," Betty corrected. "It's like two words. First word 'Melba,' second word 'lean.' Then you put it together. Melbalean."

I quirked a brow. "Got it. But what's Cotton and Cobwebs?"

My other cousin, Cordelia, with her flowing blond hair and penchant for no-nonsense, strolled in. She opened the fridge and said, "Cotton and Cobwebs is a county fair slash magical festival that happens here every year at the end of the summer. It's a big deal."

"Oh yeah," Amelia added, her gaze bright. "There's all kinds of things—rides, contests, magical pie throwing. It's so much fun."

Betty sliced the air dangerously with the knife. She wasn't a very big woman, but what she lacked in size she made up for in attitude. "For years, Melbalean always won the magical animal contest. Always. That old bat likes to think she can grow the best animals, teach them tricks and then have them win that stupid contest. Remember two years ago when she trained that squirrel to bat its eyelashes like a big baby? Stupid thing charmed the whole town."

"I take it you weren't pleased," I said.

"The only reason Melbalean wins is because she wears those pantyhose with the lines in the back. Men can't resist them."

I hid a laugh behind my hand. "Pantyhose with a line in them?"

Betty nodded. "Melbalean's a hussy. If she stepped one foot inside a Baptist church, the place would explode."

My eyebrows shot to peaks. "Don't let the Catholics get a hold of her then. But that's some pretty serious hussiness."

"You better believe it," Betty said. "But this is my ace in the hole.

Ordered this beauty special delivery and I've been waiting weeks to get it."

"You might want to open the box before whatever it is punches a hole through it," Amelia said.

"Good thinking. It might be hungry too."

"I hope it doesn't eat people," Amelia said.

Cordelia shot her an annoyed look.

Amelia shrugged. "It's shaking the box like there's no tomorrow. There's no telling what's inside."

Cordelia looked wary. "Good point."

Betty sliced the top and set the knife aside. She folded the flaps. A red comb poked out, followed by two black beady eyes.

Betty dipped her hands in the box. "Help me, will you?"

I pulled the cardboard away, noting what looked like a bag of feed in the bottom. Betty tugged, revealing a ball of golden feathers. She plopped the animal on the table and grinned proudly.

"Girls, let me present to you the winner of this year's magical creatures category at the Cotton and Cobwebs Festival."

The chicken stared blankly at us. It jutted out its head and flapped its wings. I shot a look to Amelia and Cordelia, who met my gaze.

The three of us burst into laughter.

"Is that a chicken?" I asked.

"No, it's a Holly Hobbie doll," Betty snapped.

I laughed again. Once for my stupid question—of course, it was a chicken, but also because Holly Hobbie dolls were so 1975, or whatever, and I was twenty-five. I was surprised I even knew what Holly Hobbie was.

"Laugh, girls. Laugh as much as you want, but I ordered this here chicken because it's going to win me that contest."

"How?" Amelia said. "What's it do?"

Betty stroked the animal's head like it was a cat. Now, I could talk to animals and hear their thoughts, but all I was getting from this chicken was a low-frequency hum. I'm not saying the bird wasn't of a high enough intelligence to communicate, because I was still pretty new when it came to animal speak, but I kinda felt like the hen might have fluff in its head.

So I guess what I meant was, I didn't think the animal was smart enough to communicate with me. Which was funny, because there were birds that chattered to me at the pet shop I'd inherited from my uncle, Familiar Place.

Oh, I guess I haven't explained all that yet.

My name's Pepper Dunn and I'm a witch. Found out about that recently, actually. I also inherited from my Great Uncle Donovan what's supposed to be the most important shop in all the magical town of Magnolia Cove, Alabama—the familiar store, where I match witches with their pet familiars.

If this all sounds confusing don't worry, I was confused when I first landed in town, too. But I'm getting used to it. Slowly, but surely.

And now I was staring at a chicken that was supposed to be an ace in the hole for some contest.

Betty stroked the bird's head. "Girls, this bird might not look like much, but I ordered it because of what it can lay."

"Eggs?" Amelia said.

"Not just any eggs," Betty said, "but magical eggs."

I nodded in admiration. "Magical eggs? What do they do?"

Betty smiled widely when she said, "This chicken lays silver eggs."

There was a long pause in the room until I broke it. "Silver eggs?"

Betty agreed. "That's right, silver eggs. This year, Melbalean can shove whatever animal she has right up her tush. There's no way she's beating me."

Cordelia studied the bird. "Exactly how much did you pay for a hen that lays silver eggs?"

Betty lifted her chin proudly and said, "Nine dollars and ninety-nine cents."

Another long pause before the three of us burst into laughter.

Cordelia raked her fingers through her hair. "You're kidding, right?"

"Nine ninety-nine," Amelia choked. "Are you sure it doesn't lay paper eggs?"

Betty glared at me. "And what do you have to say about it?"

I hid behind my coffee, taking an incredibly long sip before I squeaked out, "It does seem a little low. Are you paying that much in maybe five installments? Or did you order the chicken from the As-Seen-On-TV aisle at Walmart?"

"Laugh all you want, girls, but this chicken is going to win me a blue ribbon. Just you wait and see."

The kitchen door swung open and in walked two towering redheads. Now, I was a redhead and so were Cordelia and Amelia, though they bleached their hair. If Betty didn't have gray curls she might've been one too, but these two women had fiery hair—one had long, voluptuous waves and the other had straight, silky tresses.

"Good morning," my aunt Mint said. She tucked a wavy strand behind an ear.

"Y'all are up early," my other aunt, Licky, short for Licorice, said.

Betty jabbed a finger at them. "You two, get out. Whatever mischief you have in mind, you can just scat right now. I don't want any part of it."

Mint splayed a hand over her heart. "Mama, is that any way to greet your children?"

Betty hugged the chicken to her chest. "If by children you mean you two troublemakers, then yes. I want you out before lightning strikes my house or the earth eats it alive."

"You mean like in *Carrie*?" Amelia said.

"Hmm? What?" Betty said.

I shook my head. "I don't think she knows that reference."

"Oh," Amelia said, "I can tell you all about *Carrie* if you want me to."

Betty ignored her. "Like I said, trouble follows you two around like stink on poop. I don't know what you need, but it better be quick and then y'all can be on your merry way."

Aunt Licky looked at Mint. "Do you think we'll really be merry? That's a pretty jovial word."

Mint looked happy. "I think we'll be merry."

"Knock it off, you two," Betty said.

When I first arrived in Magnolia Cove, my aunts had been on an around the world trip that apparently Amelia and Cordelia had sent them on because these two grown women were serious troublemakers. But now they had returned and had barely been in town a month. Every time they stopped by, Betty was convinced the house was going to get hexed, so she shooed them right out the door before they had a chance to catch their breaths.

"Mama," Mint said, "We're here on official town business."

"At seven am on a Saturday?" Betty said, "I seriously doubt it."

Licky hiked up onto the counter and sat. "Oh, it's true. Official business."

Betty wagged a finger at her. "Don't you go getting germs all over my clean kitchen."

Licky rolled her eyes and dropped to the floor. "We're in charge of the Cotton and Cobwebs Festival."

Betty fisted a hand on her hip. "Now why would anyone put you in charge of anything?"

Mint smiled brightly. She spoke with an enthusiasm that bordered on childlike glee. "We convinced the committee that we've changed. We no longer bring chaos wherever we go."

Betty rolled her eyes. "I'll believe it when I see it. Besides, the festival isn't for another month."

"Not anymore," Mint countered. "The festival starts today."

Betty nearly threw the chicken in the air. "What?"

Mint nodded. "Yep. We decided we couldn't wait another month for all the fun, so it officially opens at noon. We came to deliver your welcome package."

Betty snatched an envelope from her hands. "This chicken won't be ready. You two," she snapped at her daughters. "Always making my life difficult. If this chicken doesn't lay an egg at the festival and Melbalean wins, you owe me my money."

Licky crossed her arms. "I'm sure it'll be fine." She rubbed her fingers over the dimple in her chin.

Mattie, the talking cat, sauntered into the room. She had short gray fur and bright green eyes. "What's all the commotion in here? Cain't a cat get some sleep?"

The chicken took one look at the cat and apparently thought *predator.* She flapped her wings so hard that she flew right out of Betty's hands and landed on the linoleum in a flurry of feathers.

"Get that bird," Betty yelled.

Mint and Licky screeched as the chicken clucked and strutted. Betty lunged for the hen, but the animal dodged right as if she was a trained escape artist. The bird ran circles around the table, kicking up a stew of feathers. I could've made a pillow out of what was molting into the air.

"Ah, all the feathers," Amelia choked. "I need air." She flew to the door and pulled it open. She inhaled a deep breath. "That's better."

"The chicken," Betty yelled.

The magical silver-egg-laying hen flapped her golden wings. She flew straight up, sailed over the table and headed through the open door.

We all stared as the chicken disappeared from sight.

Betty pointed in the hen's direction. "Well? What are y'all doing catching flies with your open mouths? We gotta go out there and get my chicken."

I stood dumbstruck for half a second before I toed on a pair of sneakers I'd laid by the door. Wearing my housecoat and armed with a cup of coffee, I marched outside to catch a hen.

Just another day with my family.

TWO

$\mathcal{C}$hicken Little ran right into the middle of town square. Magnolia Cove is small. Bubbling Cauldron Road, the main street with all the prime shops, including mine, sat only a few blocks from Betty's house.

And the chicken had a head start.

Streamers and red and white banners decorated Bubbling Cauldron. I paused, glanced in astonishment at the words Cotton and Cobwebs blazing in fire-licking letters on a floating banner over the road.

"Whoa, that is so cool," I mused.

Betty grabbed my arm. "No time to dally, kid. You've got a chicken to sweet talk."

I locked my knees. "Me? Did you see the talons on that thing? It'll rip out my eyes."

Betty dragged me with the brute strength of a superhero. "If anyone can communicate with it, it's you. Hurry. We need to catch it before Melbalean sees. There's no way I'm giving that old battle-ax a jump on me."

I tripped in my sneakers, barely catching myself from falling onto the sopping grass. It had been raining for three straight days. The ground was heavy and the air so muggy that the humidity caused sweat to pop up on my skin.

"Betty, that chicken is a straight-up bird brain. It doesn't talk. I didn't get one sense that the creature knows how to communicate with anyone other than chickens."

"That's because you don't understand it. It's a delicate hen."

I smirked. "Has to be, right? Otherwise, you wasted ten bucks?"

"I don't appreciate your sarcasm."

"I don't appreciate being dragged through the mud by a little old lady who thinks she's the Hulk."

Betty pulled a corncob pipe from her pocket and stuck it in her mouth. "How about Popeye?"

I stifled a laugh. I caught a flutter of feathers in my peripheral vision. "There's the hen. She's at those booths."

Betty snarled. "Great. There's Melbalean the horrible."

I blinked. At one of the booths, I saw a little woman with a hunchback and thick glasses. She wore a floral dress and white Keds.

I stared harder. "That sweet little lady is Melbalean the horrible?"

Betty snapped her fingers and her pipe sparked. "Don't let the glasses fool you. Underneath that wrinkled exterior is a cunning predator."

Okay.

The hen fluttered up into the air, flapping its wings right into Melbalean's open arms.

"Great," Betty said. "Now she's got it."

We strolled up to Melbalean, who was cooing into the chicken's ear. Wait. Do chickens have ears?

The hen cocked its head at us. Well, they've got beady little eyes. That much is for sure.

"Betty Craple," Melbalean said, pronouncing the last name like Crapple, with two p's. "Why are you here so early? And barely dressed."

Betty held out her arms. "I would kindly thank you for handing me my chicken. And you know very well my name rhymes with maple."

Melbalean stroked the hen's head. "This pretty thing is yours? Then why's she running away from you?"

"Because it's none of your business, that's why."

"We got her in the mail," I offered.

Betty gave me the stink eye to end all stink eyes.

I shrugged. "What? It's true."

"You don't offer the enemy any information," Betty whispered.

I had a really hard time seeing the sweet little Melbalean as anything other than harmless.

"You're a little chicken, aren't you?" Melbalean cooed in its ear.

"Hand her over," Betty said.

"Well, of course, I'll hand over this ten dollar silver-egg-laying chicken," Melbalean said.

Betty's eyes grew to the size of saucers. "What did you say?"

Melbalean pursed her lips. "I said, I will gladly give you the hen you paid nine dollars and ninety-nine cents for. You know, the one that lays silver eggs."

"Sorcery," Betty whispered.

Melbalean rolled her eyes. "If you'd paid five more dollars, you could've bought the golden-egg-laying chicken like I did. But you didn't because you're too cheap."

Melbalean dropped Betty's hen onto her booth's counter and picked up a cage. In it strutted a hen with silvery feathers.

"Lays golden eggs," Melbalean said.

I flared out my arms. "Wait. So okay." I pointed to Betty. "You bought a ten dollar chicken that lays silver eggs and you," I directed toward Melbalean, "purchased one that lays golden eggs."

"That's right," Melbalean said.

I smacked my lips. "It sounds to me as if both of you were taken for a ride. Who the heck would sell chickens that lay precious metals?"

Both women blinked at me as if I was stupid-is-as-stupid-does. Eventually, Betty turned to Melbalean. "My chicken's going to lay more eggs than yours, so watch out, old lady."

Wow. Talk about the pot calling the kettle black. Betty was so old she might as well be aging in reverse instead of forward.

Does that make sense?

It does to me. That's all that matters, I suppose.

Melbalean shooed Betty's hen off her booth. "You better hurry up and catch that bird. Judging starts tonight and it looks like your hen's going to need time to acclimate. You know, so she can lay an egg."

Melbalean's hen let out a cry. "Oh, what do we have here?"

She unhinged the cage and stuck her hand beneath the hen. "Well, I don't believe it—could it be?" She pulled out her hand and opened her fingers. A small shiny golden egg lay in the center of her palm. "Why, it sure is. A golden egg! You better get a move on, Betty, if you're going to win this year. You'll need a whole mountain of silver eggs to beat my gold."

Betty pulled her pipe from her mouth and spat on the floor. "It's probably wrapped in yellow foil." She took my arm. "Come on, Pepper. Let's get my new hen home and get her laying some eggs."

We walked back. Betty huffed with every step. "I should've known that old battle-ax would try to outdo me," she snarled. "We've got a lot of work ahead of us when we get to the house."

"We?" I said. "I've got a shop to open in a few hours."

Betty smiled brightly. "Great idea. We'll take the chicken to Familiar Place. See if being around the other animals helps warm her up to us. Maybe they can teach you how to talk to her."

A knot of unease twisted my belly. "Wait. No. I'm not getting involved in this."

Betty batted her eyelashes at me. "But we're family."

My heart tightened. Betty, my cousins and my aunts were all the family I had in the world. The best way to manipulate me was to remind me of that fact and guilt me about it, which clearly wasn't that hard since all Betty had to do was mention the word "family" and unease automatically flooded my body.

I sighed. "Okay. You can bring the hen to the shop. But with this festival starting today, I'm guessing we'll be getting in a lot of out-of-towners, and that means I'll be busy."

"Great," Betty said, "I'll jump in the shower with the hen and I'll see you at the store."

Wait. What?

"You always run around town in your robe?"

The voice came from the side. I hadn't heard it in a good solid week, and my heart thundered because of it.

I slanted my head and caught a pair of blue eyes peeking out from under long, dark lashes. A handsome face with a straight nose, an easy smile that revealed a dimple in the right cheek, and a bit of scruff along the jaw all belonged to Axel Reign, Magnolia Cove's one and only private detective.

His shoulder length hair was pulled back, making him look kind of like a mix between a superhero and, well, a superhero.

We stopped. Axel nodded at Betty. "Miss Craple."

She wagged a finger at him. "Don't you *Miss Craple* me. Your intentions with my granddaughter better be pure."

A hint of red flushed his cheeks. "Ah, well. Good to see you, too."

She snorted. "You bet your bottom dollar it's good to see me. Seeing me means we're all still here alive on earth."

"That's not what that means," I said. "It means *you're* still alive on earth."

Betty shrugged. "You'd be surprised." She glanced toward the festival. "I don't have all day to dilly-dally. I've got to get on this chicken and coax her into sitting a mountain of eggs. I'll see you two later."

I waved. "Okay."

She shot Axel a scathing look. "And no kissing. I'll know."

I cinched my robe tighter and glanced away, hoping that I didn't die of embarrassment. After she left, I checked on Axel, who stood studying me.

"Haven't seen you around in a while," he said.

"I've been busy. You know, with the whole owning a pet shop thing. What about you?"

He grazed a thumb along his jaw. Like, how did he manage to make the simplest thing look so sexy?

"I've been keeping busy. Had a job out of town that's kept me away. Ran into your friend Rufus."

I cleared my throat. "Not my friend."

And he wasn't. The mysterious Rufus had first appeared in my life several weeks ago before I ever arrived in Magnolia Cove. He'd demanded that I come with him or die. Let me tell you, I would've been toast if it hadn't been for Mattie the Cat. She saved my butt and guided me to my new home.

Of course, if that had been the end of it, the whole Rufus thing wouldn't have been much of a story. Problem is, one night I tried to sneak out of Magnolia Cove and Rufus was waiting. If it hadn't been for Axel, I probably would've been *burned* toast.

So I owed Axel. Big time.

Axel nodded. "I know. Rufus was being investigated for turning a person into a toad and refusing to turn him back."

I grimaced. "That's horrible."

Did I forget to mention that according to Axel, Rufus had a penchant for playing Dr. Frankenstein?

"I found the guy, saved him, but he had no memory of who'd turned him into a frog."

A cool wind blew my hair in my eyes. I raked it from my face. "So once again, the mysterious Rufus gets away with committing acts of evil."

"Yep."

Another strand of hair flicked onto my lips. Axel brushed it away before I had a chance to. The air stilled as an electric jolt snaked along my skin. I swallowed.

Axel retreated a step. He shoved his hands into his pockets.

Right. There was a galaxy of tension between the two of us, but we couldn't act on it.

I *guess* we couldn't. I was dumped a few weeks ago by my boyfriend, and Axel said he had stuff going on—which I took to mean there was another woman.

Before the tension grew weirder, I decided to break away. "Well, I guess I'll be seeing you."

He cleared his throat. "Yeah. Listen, you been staying out of trouble?"

I scoffed. "Of course. I've been learning about my shop. Trying to work on my witch powers. All that good stuff."

His blue gaze leveled at me. "Want to have dinner tonight?"

I did a double take. "Um. What about all that stuff we've said?"

Axel nodded. "It won't mean anything. It's just dinner. It's not like I'm going to dress up. I might not even take a shower before."

I laughed. "Okay. Well, in that case, I'll probably wear this bathrobe. Is that okay with you?"

He smiled. "Works for me."

A chicken clucked in the background and I turned to look. Melbalean was pulling another egg from under the hen.

"Ugh. I'd better get home. Betty is determined to beat that woman."

Axel stared at Melbalean for a moment. "So I see you've met her already."

I quirked a brow. "Who, Melbalean? Yeah. Betty's all ticked off at her. I've already had to separate those two. Make sure they didn't kill each other. Why?"

Axel's gaze darkened. "Because Melbalean Mayes is Rufus's mother."

Well holy sack of shrimp and grits. That was a bombshell I didn't expect.

THREE

"You've got to win this contest," I said.

I stood in the center of my pet store. I'd showered, dressed and was having a pow-wow with Betty. It was about thirty minutes to opening.

She tugged on the waistband of her pants, pulling them up to below her boobs. "So you've seen things my way."

I tapped the edge of my third cup of coffee. "Melbalean is Rufus's mother?"

Betty nodded. "Yep. She had him in her forties. Rufus was an accident. Melbalean always coddled that boy. She's kept him from being arrested about a thousand times, even though he's obviously trouble on a stick."

I smirked. "All I know is that he has attacked me twice, so I'm not a fan." I flashed her a bright smile. "Which means I'll gladly help you."

Betty pulled the chicken from the box and put her on the counter. The animals in the pet shop saw the new arrival and immediately started chirping.

"Who's that?" meowed one of the kittens.

"It looks like a chicken," cried one of the puppies.

"It's a hen," cawed a parrot.

"I bet it tastes like chicken," said a kitten. "That's my favorite thing to eat."

I patted the air. "First of all, y'all eat pet food. You've never eaten chicken. Secondly, will y'all please be quiet? We're trying to work, here."

The animals settled and I glanced from the chicken, who was pecking and strutting, to Betty. I gave her a questioning look. "So what exactly is it you want me to do?"

Betty gestured toward the hen. "Get her comfortable enough to lay eggs. Lots of eggs."

I grimaced. "I'm not sure I can, but I'll try."

"You're the animal whisperer. If anyone can do it, it's you."

I rolled my eyes. My family's faith in my abilities far outweighed my own trust. But hey, I was willing to try. If nothing else, it would hopefully give Betty a glimmer of a chance of beating Melbalean.

I'll be honest, being new to the whole witch thing, I didn't really know *how* to talk to animals. The truth was, their voices just popped into my head. Yes, I know I'm not crazy because...well, I don't really know, but I trust that it's animals I hear.

Anyway, before I started contemplating the rabbit hole of my sanity, I shifted my focus to Chicken Little.

I focused on her and listened.

Zilch. Nada. Nothing.

Not one thought. Since focusing on her didn't seem to work, I pushed my thoughts out and encouraged the hen to lay beautiful silver eggs.

She clucked and fluttered her wings. Then she settled on the floor. *CLUUUUUUUKAAAAA!*

I shot Betty a terrified look. My grandmother jumped in the air— silver curls and all. Betty did a little dance that incorporated pointing invisible guns toward the sky and firing them. "You did it, kid. Got her to lay. Now, let's see what's underneath."

Betty reached down. The hen shifted for her and Betty revealed a silvery egg. "Ha! Here it is. Now, all I need is a mountain of them and I'll have that old witch beat."

"Can I see it?" I said.

She handed it to me. The egg was light. Really light. Like it was pumped with air. I tapped it on the counter and said, "I don't think this is silver. I think it's aluminum."

Betty's eyebrows shot to peaks. "What?"

"I'm no expert, but it's too light to be silver. I mean, Betty, you bought the bird for ten dollars. Did you really think it would lay silver eggs?"

Betty snatched it from me. She sniffed the egg, scratched at it and finally declared, "Well if this is aluminum, what's Melbalean got?"

I shrugged. "Can't be real gold."

Betty rubbed her chin. "Must be fool's gold. Ha! I'll still beat her because my eggs are an actual metal that's worth something. She's got a worthless fifteen dollar hen!"

"The hen might be hungry after laying an egg. I imagine that takes a lot of energy," I said.

Betty raised a bag. "Her food is right here. Came with her."

I found a bowl and filled it with feed. The hen pecked at it hungrily, jutting out her neck and clucking.

Betty mumbled on about the egg. "My ace in the hole." My grand-mother displayed the egg for the chicken. "You did good, girl. Now I need you to lay more."

The hen clucked and fixed its beady eyes on the egg. In half a second, the bird had fluttered up and was trying to hook its talons into Betty's arm. It squawked and screeched as a whirlwind of feathers kicked up in the shop.

"It's attacking," cried one of the kittens. "Kill it and eat it!"

I ducked as the bird flogged Betty.

My grandmother kept a straight face as she reached out her hand and yanked the hen by the neck. The bird continued flapping, almost manic in its attack.

"What happened?" I said.

Betty thrust the hen out, far enough away that it couldn't hurt her. "I don't think she liked me taking her egg."

"Or pressuring her," I offered.

"Or that. See if you can calm her."

I bit down my instinct to argue and concentrated on serene thoughts. The bird continued flapping and kicking.

"It's not working," I said.

"Help me get her in the box."

"You really need a cage."

"Everybody's an expert. I'll get one later."

I grabbed the box and held it open while Betty dropped the hen inside. I closed the flaps, but the bird continued to scuffle against the cardboard.

"Wow. She's not quieting down, is she?"

Betty grabbed the box, which jerked almost from her hands. "I'm taking this home. I'll whip up some feed with something calming in it and give it to her. Hopefully, she'll be ready for the festival tonight."

I opened the door for her. "Good luck. I'll see you there."

Betty pinpointed a sharp glare at me. "Stores close at three during the Cotton and Cobwebs Festival."

"They do?"

Betty nodded. "Sure do. So that owners can enjoy the festivities."

I nodded back. "Okay, great."

As she was leaving, my aunts Licky and Mint strolled in. Betty pointed a finger at them. "And don't let these two talk you into doing anything stupid."

"Good to see you too, Mama," Mint said, flicking her loose red curls over one shoulder.

"Bah! Because of you I almost lost my chicken."

Licky blew her a kiss. "We would've helped you find her."

Betty opened her mouth to say something, but then shut it and left.

Mint smiled at me. It was a wide, friendly smile. My aunts looked a lot alike, but Mint had a long, angular face and Licky, who had the silky straight hair, had more of a round face with the chin dimple.

Mint wrapped me up in a hug. "Hugging you is like hugging your mom. Anyone ever told you that?"

A swell of pride rushed inside me. "No. Not ever, and I'll take it as a compliment."

My mother, Sassafras, had died in childbirth, and after her death, my father had elected not to tell me about my witch heritage. He died a couple of years ago from cancer. I missed him, and luckily my new family helped fill that void.

Licky gave me another hug. "We're so glad to have this time to get to know you. We've missed you your whole life."

I laughed. "I guess I missed y'all too, even though I never knew you."

Mint grabbed my hand. "You know we're running the festival this year."

"A lot of responsibility," Licky added.

"It barely gives us time to do anything while the festival is going on," Mint said.

"We'll be so busy," Licky said.

"There's so much to see and do," Mint said.

I nodded, trying to piece together the whirlwind of their conversation. "I'm sure. I can't wait to experience it."

Fact was, Axel had texted that after dinner he'd escort me around the festival, which I was pretty excited about.

But of course, I wanted to play it cool. Even though we were spending time at the fair, it didn't mean anything.

Right. I'll keep telling myself that.

"Anyway," Mint said, her gaze bobbing around the shop, "there's a lot of stuff we can't do."

"Because we'll be so busy," Licky said.

"Sure, I understand."

"We could use an assistant," Mint said.

"But we don't have time to find anyone," Licky finished.

"So we're stuck," Mint said.

"I don't understand," I said.

"There's this one booth that's always sold out in about five minutes," Mint said.

"Every night," Licky said.

"It never fails," Mint added.

"What is it?" I said.

Mint leaned forward conspiratorially. "Well, since you asked, we have to tell you. Old Leona Doodle is a food witch. Has a restaurant in a cave down in Hollyhock Hollow. She comes up for the festival every year and brings her kitchen along."

"Food is to die for," Licky said.

"But you see we'll be so busy with festivities we won't be able to get any," Mint said. "And it's that way every night she's there."

"And she makes the best baked macaroni and cheese you've ever tasted," Licky said.

"But it's always gone in about five minutes."

"She sells out completely."

I glanced from one shining face to the other until dawn cracked in my brain. "You want me to get you some?"

Mint's face broke into a beaming smile. "Would you?"

I nodded happily. "Sure. Whatever you need. Y'all are family, after all. I know everyone says y'all are full of mischief, but I haven't seen it."

Licky squeezed my arm. "Most of the time it's a big misunderstanding. Just happens that way. After all, Mint and I are simple organizational witches."

The door to Familiar Place opened. The bell tinkled overhead. A woman and her young daughter entered.

I glanced at Licky. "I've never heard of organizational witches."

Mint headed toward the door. "We love organization. We collect and put things together by size, shape, whatever—that's what we do best."

I smiled. "So you'll be perfect for the festival."

"Yep," Licky said. "Listen, we see you're getting busy, so we'll leave."

They left, and I turned my attention to the woman and her daughter. "Welcome to Familiar Place. How can I help you?"

I FINISHED up my day at three and headed to the house for a late lunch.

After feeding the animals and tucking them in for the night, my stomach was growling something fierce. I passed Castin' Iron, where several large iron skillets zoomed about outside. These skillets weren't for cooking; they were for riding.

That's right. In Magnolia Cove, witches didn't ride brooms. Instead, we rode broom-length cast iron skillets.

It was awesome.

Theodora and Harry, the shop owners, waved as I passed.

"How's your skillet doing?" Harry called.

I gave him a thumb's up. "Great."

"Glad I could sell it to you," he said.

Theodora glared at him. "You know good and well I found the skillet that she rides. Stop taking all the credit, old man."

"Woman, you will be the death of me," Harry said.

I laughed as I headed home. The small picket fence screeched as I entered. The guard-vine flowing across the porch dipped and gave me a good sniff. I patted the red bud.

"Hi there, Jennie. It's just me."

Jennie recoiled back across the ceiling and let me enter. "I'm home," I called out.

Betty, Amelia and Cordelia sat at the table, finishing up what looked like a light lunch of chicken salad and crackers.

No one said anything when I entered. I dropped my purse on the chair. "Why's everyone so quiet?"

Amelia and Cordelia shot Betty a look.

"Word around town is that Melbalean's bird is laying real gold eggs," Betty said.

I plopped at the table and picked up a plate. "I don't believe it. I'm sure that's not true."

Betty's eyes shifted from my cousins to me. "These two won't help me."

Cordelia pushed her long hair from her face. "She wants us to steal one of the eggs and see."

Amelia bit into a cracker. "Yeah. In front of everyone, our grandmother wants us to snatch an egg. We'll be thrown out of the festival."

21

I scooped up a dollop of salad and plated it, pushing the grapes out. Why did people make chicken salad with grapes? Not my favorite combination.

"You could always get Licky and Mint to do it. I'm sure they'd be up for it."

Betty shook her head. "Those two would screw up boiling water. We'll be lucky if half the town isn't burned down before the festival is over."

Amelia shrugged. "Well, I'm not stealing an egg. I'm not getting arrested for a harebrained scheme."

Betty glared at her. She snapped her fingers and a Rolodex flared to life.

Amelia rolled her eyes. Cordelia stifled a laugh behind her hand. According to Betty, the Rolodex was chock full of eligible bachelors all suitable for Amelia's attention.

Images of profiles and a blur of pictures flitted in the air above us. The shuffling finally stopped on an image of a young man with a shock of black hair brushed into a pompadour. He smiled so brightly you could see a diamond of light sparkling on his teeth. He stood in front of a mountain and wore a thick parka.

"Who's that?" Amelia said.

Betty glared at her. "Lane Longmire. He's an adventure hunter. Been searching the Himalayas for the Abominable Snowman."

"I think you mean yeti," Cordelia said. "They live in the Himalayas."

Betty snapped her fingers and Cordelia's plate vanished. "That's what you get for back talking."

"I was finished anyway."

Amelia's eyes gleamed at the picture.

Betty smiled like a copperhead about to kill a field mouse. "He's handsome, isn't he?" she said.

Amelia wiped a line of drool from her bottom lip. She glanced furtively at Betty. "He's okay."

Betty smacked her lips. "Don't be such a phony. He's hot and you know it. He's handsome, loves adventure and is probably built like a stallion beneath those clothes."

"Oh dear Lord," I said.

An old woman talking about a man as if he was a piece of meat was not my idea of a good time.

"What's your point?" Amelia said. "I mean, he's good-looking, but I don't know if I'm interested in a guy who's on your dating Rolodex."

Betty leaned over and said, "What if I told you he was on his way here to meet you?"

Amelia threw up her hands. "What?"

Betty laughed. "Laney boy's left the mountains and is trekking across the globe to meet you, Amelia." She glanced at her watch. "He should be here any minute."

Amelia clapped her hands and a mirror shot up in front of her. "I've got to touch up my makeup and get ready."

Betty glanced guiltily from side to side. Amelia caught it and glared at her. "What is it? What aren't you telling me?"

"You might have to do more than freshen up your makeup."

"Why?"

"Because this is the picture I sent him."

An image in a frame flared to life. Cordelia took one look at it and burst into laughter.

"What is it?" I said.

I leaned over until I could get a good look at the picture. The photo that Betty had sent Lane Longmire was nothing short of a Farrah Fawcett lookalike.

"What is this, the seventies?" Cordelia said. "Couldn't you have picked a celebrity that's at least still alive for Amelia to impersonate?"

Betty crossed her arms. "I didn't want to make it too obvious. I figured with some extensions and a little highlighter, Amelia would look like her."

I held in a laugh as Amelia shook her head. "No way. No way am I going to magic myself to look differently for some guy."

The doorbell rang.

Betty smiled brightly. "Oops. Looks like he's here. And now for the million dollar question—" she raised her hands and an orb of white light blossomed in her palm, "to change or not to change?"

All eyes fell on Amelia. She fisted her hands in front of her face and said, "This is against everything I stand for."

"You should be standing for a hot guy," Betty said.

I laughed.

"Not helping," Amelia said.

The bell rang again.

"What'll it be?" Betty said.

Amelia glanced at Lane's picture one more time before saying, "Do it. Change me."

FOUR

*W*ith a snap of Betty's fingers, Amelia went from a pixie cut and pixie-faced to long, luxurious caramel colored hair and more contouring makeup than even Kim Kardashian did on a normal day.

"Wow," I said, "you might need a makeup class to keep this up."

Amelia dragged her gaze to Betty. "Don't die anytime soon. I'm going to need your magic to keep this up."

Betty waddled to the door and opened it. On the other side stood Lane Longmire. No joke. I thought maybe it might not be him, but sure enough, it was the mountaineer himself.

"Hey there," he said in a long Southern drawl—the kind that either sent a girl running for the hills like her hair was on fire or turned her to a puddle at his feet.

I was the sort of Southern gal who liked men to have a smooth accent and Lane's was to die for.

His gaze immediately swept to Amelia. "You must be Amelia," he said. "It's a pleasure to meet you."

"Same here," she said.

Betty boobed her way between them. "I'm Betty Craple and these are my other granddaughters, Cordelia and Pepper."

He dipped his head. "Nice to meet y'all."

Betty grinned at him. "Lane, why don't you come in and have a nice glass of tea? Sit a while."

I excused myself to my room so I could get ready for my date—sorry, not a date. So I could get ready for dinner and a stroll around the fair with Axel.

Mattie stretched in the window seat when I entered. "Sugar, what's all that there commotion downstairs?"

I shucked off my shoes. "Betty wants me to steal an egg from Melbalean and she's found Amelia a new boyfriend. He chases magical creatures for a living."

"Sounds like a typical Saturday."

I showered and dressed, killing time until the sun started to sink into the horizon. By the time I padded downstairs, Betty was waiting for me with the chicken in the box.

"I see she settled down," I said.

She shook her head. "Not really. I had to put a sleeping spell on it. Hopefully, I didn't overdo it and kill the hen."

"Let's hope not," I said.

"Come on. You gotta help me set up for the competition."

I frowned. "Isn't it hours away?"

Betty shrugged. "Never hurts to get an edge on. Melbalean's already there."

"Good point. Where's everybody else?"

Betty waddled toward the door. "Amelia and her new boyfriend went to look around town. Cordelia's already gone to the fair. So it's you and me. We gotta steal one of Melbalean's eggs. You coming?"

I glanced at my watch.

"Don't worry," she said, "I already told your boyfriend to meet us at the fair."

I shook my head. "I don't have a boyfriend."

"Not officially." She opened the door and walked through. "Come on. I'm not getting any younger."

When we reached the festival, the celebration was in high swing. It looked like half the town had swooped on it. There were competition booths of all sorts set up on one side, and magical rides and games set up on the other.

My gaze dragged over a bucking cast iron skillet. The sign read that if you stayed on a full sixty seconds, you won the skillet.

Slap me upside the head and call me stupid, but the last thing I wanted was a bucking skillet. Heck, I had my own and didn't want to try to tame another.

But the line for the skillet wound around the ride. So clearly I was in the minority.

We wove through the people milling about. Mint and Licky sat at the ticket booth, charging folks to come in. Licky saw me and waved. I waved back.

"You should stay away from those two," Betty said.

"They're your daughters," I said.

Betty nodded. "I know. So it's expert opinion I'm giving you. Your mother was nothing like them. She was normal, sweet. Those two are something else."

I sighed out a shot of air and followed Betty until we reached her booth. It was less than three feet from Melbalean's.

Melbalean glanced over and smiled. "You're back. My golden girl here has already laid half a dozen eggs today. I'm stashing them in the corner to make sure no one steals them." Her gaze roved over Betty's hen. "If I were you, I wouldn't worry about hiding your eggs. Why have silver when you can have gold, I always say."

"Because gold is a bitter, nasty metal that's useless in a spell," Betty snapped. "Every witch knows if you want to work a real spell you need silver."

"Or aluminum," I said quietly.

Her gaze darted to me and I shrugged. "Sorry."

She tugged me to the side. "The judging isn't until later. I'll keep an eye out and when Melbalean's distracted, I'll whistle for you."

I cocked my head. "What if I'm on the other side of the fair?"

"I'll do it really loud, like this." Betty crammed her fingers in her mouth and let out a shrill that nearly burst my eardrum.

I cringed. "Ow."

"Don't worry, only you can hear that."

I wrung out my ear with the tip of my finger. "Good thing." My gaze darted around the fair until I saw Axel striding toward us. His lips curled when our eyes met. My knees wobbled.

The smell of pine soap wafted off him when he reached us. His hair was damp and hung around his shoulders.

"Sorry, I'm late. I had a last minute call that tied me up," he said.

I twisted a strand of my hair absentmindedly. "No worries. After all, Betty changed the arrangement on you. She told me."

He raked his fingers through his locks and said, "Who am I to argue with her?"

She wagged a finger at him. "You're darned right. If everyone in the world listened to me, the earth would be a happier place."

"Or a crazier one," I said.

Betty placed her fingers over her mouth. "Remember the signal."

I smirked. "Don't worry."

I'd have to be deaf to forget it.

"Can we bring you anything?" Axel asked her.

Betty scratched her chin. "I'd like some of Leona's shrimp and grits, if she brought it. If not, some peach cobbler."

Axel agreed. "Done."

We left Betty as she opened the box and was doing her best to coax the chicken awake. I saw her tap its beak and the bird fluttered to life, taking its perch on a nesting bed that had been made for it.

Axel's hand slid down my arm until he was holding my hand.

"What're you doing?" I said.

"Touching you." He paused. "Is that okay?"

I felt heat burn my cheeks as his gaze rested on me. "As long as it doesn't mean anything."

"Don't worry," he said. "So. What would you like to do first? Play a game? Go through a magical maze? Get ice cream?"

I clicked my tongue and remembered my promise to Licky and Mint. "What about Leona's?"

Axel shook his head. "She won't open for a while."

"Okay, because I'm supposed to pick up some of her baked macaroni and cheese, too."

Axel laughed. "Don't worry, we'll have plenty of time for that. You want dinner?"

I tipped my head from side to side. "I'm okay right now."

He grinned at me. "All right. So what'll it be first?"

I thought about it. "How about the magical maze?"

"Always a wise choice."

We stood outside a rectangular blue building with the name Mysteries of the Universe in white painted across the top. Clapboards made up the sides and top. The pieces flipped and turned soundlessly, constantly changing the shape of the structure.

"Why's it doing that?" I said.

Axel's warm smile sent a jolt of energy straight to my core. "Because once inside, the walls move."

I quirked a brow. "They do?"

"Oh yes," he said in a mysterious voice. "This is no ordinary maze. This one is alive."

I stifled a giggle behind my hand. "Really?"

"You still game?" he said.

I nodded. "Sure. How many opportunities will I have in my life to be inside something like this?"

"A lot if you stay in Magnolia Cove," he said.

"How about we both pretend this is a one-shot deal?"

His hand squeezed mine as he said, "Sounds good to me."

Fifteen minutes later, I was laughing and holding madly to Axel as we wove around walls that disappeared when touched, walls that moved and walls that were invisible.

Oh, and did I mention the whole thing was timed? If you didn't make it out within the deadline, you had to do the whole thing over.

It was like being stuck in a deranged person's nightmare.

I stopped running and inhaled a deep shot of air. "What sort of insane person created this thing? We have to run, but if I do I'll break my nose on a wall I can't see."

Axel smiled. "Don't worry, I can see them."

I narrowed my gaze. "How can you see them when I can't?"

He opened his mouth, perfect teeth shining through. "I just can."

I tipped my head toward him. "Secrets, Mr. Reign?"

He ignored me and glanced at his watch. "One minute left to escape. If not, we start over."

I faced forward again. "Okay. Come on. Let's get out of here." As cool as the concept was, I didn't want to be stuck in the maze for the rest of the day.

We dashed through the last portion and burst outside. Cool wind struck my face, sending my skin tingling. I'd worked up a sweat inside, and I wiped the hair plastered to my face away. Great. First sort of date with Axel and here I was looking like a hot mess.

"Want some ice cream?" he said.

I glanced at the little booth he was pointing to and said, "No, but I'll take a sweet tea."

Axel nodded toward an empty bench under a willow and said, "Rest for a second. I'll be back."

I watched him jog away as I took a seat. My gaze drifted over the festival goers. I noticed Betty kept a solid eye on Mclbalean, who stood talking to some folks. I could almost see the glimmer of lust in Betty's eye at the gold laying hen.

Pretty soon she'd be whistling for me. How was I going to explain that to Axel?

Hmm. Deal with it when it happened, I guess.

I also spotted Amelia, aka Farrah Fawcett with her new beau. I had to say, they made a dashing couple even if Amelia's hair was fake. They looked good together.

Axel sat, and I scooched over, giving him more room. "Here's your tea."

I took the sweating paper cup. "Thanks."

A long sip of sugary goodness made everything right in the world. I opened my purse and pulled out a bag of jelly beans that my cousin Carmen—my second cousin—made at her sweet store. I opened the lid and dropped a handful in.

Axel's eyebrows shot to peaks. "Adding more sugar to sugar?"

"I like my sugar comas to be well deserved."

"I think you've accomplished that."

I took a sip as our eyes met. A thunderous herd of butterflies wracked against my chest as the energy buzzed between us.

Or was that the humidity?

"So how could you see the invisible walls?" I said.

Axel wedged onto the bench and stretched out one arm. "Just one of my talents."

I rolled my eyes. "*That* answers the question."

"Oh, did you want an answer?" he teased.

"I was looking for one."

"Let's say it's part of my magic."

"That's even less of an answer. Humans can't see things that aren't there." I cocked a brow at him. "Are you an alien?"

He hooted with laughter. "Far from it."

"I see this conversation's going nowhere."

Axel was quiet. He watched the crowd for a moment. "I'm a private person."

"Who likes to have company at festivals."

"I hadn't seen you in a while. I missed you."

I did a double take. "You missed me? We've only spent a little time together."

He drummed his fingers on the bench. "You grew on me quickly." His gaze sent a quivering spear straight to my heart. "I joke that our time together doesn't mean anything, but we have a connection, one that I don't want to fizzle out. You don't see someone for a while, someone you connect with, and everything you've built vanishes because inevitably someone goes in a different direction."

I took another long sip. "The only direction I'm going is to Familiar Place to wrangle a bunch of talking creatures."

He laughed. "You'd be surprised how life can change—where it can take you."

I thought back to my own life and how drastically it had changed from being fired at my waitressing job to owning my own store. "You're right about that, but it still doesn't answer my question."

He sighed. "Pepper, I've said it before—there are things about me that are too difficult to discuss."

"Becoming friends with someone means you have to let them in. We haven't known each other for very long, but we're friends. We've kissed, so that definitely puts us somewhere on that path."

Axel threw his head back in laughter.

I flicked my hair out of my eyes and said, "The last guy I dated cared about fantasy football more than he did me."

Axel's eyes darkened. "Sounds like a real jerk."

I shrugged. "Anyway, that's something about me that I don't like to tell people. Why would I? Makes me look like an idiot for dating him."

Axel rubbed my arm. "I don't like fantasy football."

I laughed. "I guess that's about as good as anything." My palms were suddenly very sweaty. I wiped them on my legs. "The humidity's getting to me."

Axel nodded. "Yeah. It's not too hot today, but still muggy." He cocked his head toward the knot of people. "Leona's is about to open. Want to head over?"

I clicked my tongue. "Sounds perfect."

The line for Leona's wasn't too long. Leona herself was a tall, wiry woman with gray hair piled up on top of her head. She had a sharp look about her that sent chills down my spine.

"She's not known for being nice," Axel whispered in my ear.

"Why are you whispering?"

"Because if she hears me, she might refuse to give you any food."

So this was Magnolia Cove's version of a school's hall monitor, or some sort of food guard. I watched as Leona heaped up globs of food into foam containers and passed them down to be rung up by the woman punching the cash register.

Axel's phone rang. He tugged it from his pocket and glanced at it. He frowned. "I need to take this. It'll be a minute."

I watched as he stepped aside, leaving me in the line.

"Well, I heard that Melbalean *knew* what Betty was bringing this year."

"You don't say."

"No, and I heard she spied on Betty. That's how she knew to buy the golden chicken."

A knot the size of Texas swelled in my gut. My eyes nearly popped from their sockets as two women directly behind me revealed secrets that made my head buzz.

And not in a good way.

I wanted to turn and look back, but I knew as soon as I did the women would shut up—and I wanted to know more.

"That rivalry goes back decades," the first woman said. "Melbalean wanted to make sure she won this year, so she found out what Betty was bringing and outdid her."

"I wouldn't tangle with Betty Craple if you paid me," the second woman whispered.

"You know that Melbalean looks innocent, but there have always been rumors that she dabbles in dark things," whispered the first woman with authority.

"That Rufus *did* have to come from somewhere," said the other woman.

So it wasn't a coincidence that Melbalean purchased the golden-egg-laying chicken. The whole situation had been rigged. I bit my lip.

I was angry. Betty had been so proud of her chicken and to see her excitement plummet had crushed my soul a little bit.

And now come to find out Melbalean planned the whole thing. She didn't deserve to win. Cheaters never win, right? I was going to make certain.

The line suddenly snapped left, and I found myself being stared at by Leona herself. She gazed at me expectantly. No hello, no nothing.

Guess her food was pretty awesome because her welcome was about as cold as a Yankee in the middle of a blizzard.

"Hmm. I need two mac and cheeses and one shrimp and grits." My gaze flickered over a pan of peach cobbler. The crust was nice and brown and the gloopy fruit concoction looked extra sugary and delicious. My stomach quivered with hunger.

"And one peach cobbler."

"Make that two," Axel said, sliding up beside me.

I slanted my head toward him. "Everything okay?"

He nodded, keeping his gaze straight ahead, which made me think everything was not okay. "Just some loose ends from the last case."

Leona heaped up the food as saliva started pooling in my mouth. "Wow. This food looks amazing."

"Best in town," Axel said. Leona slid the containers to the cashier. "I've got it," he added, pulling out his wallet.

He paid, and we were collecting the food when I said, "No wonder Licky and Mint sent me to pick it up for them. This looks amazing."

Leona stopped heaping food and turned. She cocked one beady eye at me and leaned over. "Who'd you say?"

Everyone in Leona's kitchen stopped. Their gazes swiveled to me. Heat bloomed on my cheeks.

I cleared my throat and said, "Mint and Licky."

Leona's mouth pursed into a line so thin I thought it had vanished for good. "I told those two they were never allowed to eat my food ever again." She held out her hand. "Give me those plates."

I didn't know what sin my aunts had committed to warrant Leona barring them from her kitchen, but I did know that they were my aunts, which meant they were family. There was one thing I was beginning to be protective of, and that was what family I had left in this world.

At that moment, I made an executive decision. I hugged the containers to me, glanced at Axel and said, "Run!"

FIVE

$\mathcal{W}$e raced through the festival until we reached the ticket booth, where Licky and Mint were sitting.

I put the boxes down. "We just had to beat off a fire-breathing Leona," I said, giving them both pointed looks. "Y'all care to tell me why you sent me into enemy territory without telling me?"

Licky and Mint exchanged looks full of guilt.

"I'll be over here," Axel said.

I nodded as he left me to my family.

"Don't get me wrong," I said. "I'm happy to help however I can, but y'all sent me in knowing you couldn't get any of her food, and probably got me banned from there as well." I folded my arms and glared at my aunts as if they were two grown dogs who'd pooped on the floor. "Care to tell me why?"

Mint sighed. "We accidentally set her kitchen on fire once. It wasn't our fault. It just happened."

"Uh huh," I said, unsure whether I believed the story or not. I leaned over and tried to look as intimidating as possible. "Well next time y'all want me to do a favor for you, do *me* a favor and give me the whole story first. As they say, honesty is the best policy."

Licky glanced at the floor. "We're sorry, but sometimes it's easier to ask forgiveness than permission. We also thought if we told you the truth you wouldn't do it."

"We don't want you to have a bad impression of us," Mint said.

My mouth curled into a slow smile. "It's okay. I understand. Anyway, enjoy your food. I'm going to eat some cobbler."

I grabbed the plates and found Axel off to the side. He shot me an amused smile. I tipped my chin toward him. "Are you laughing at me?"

He smiled. "Yes. I don't think I've ever seen you angry before."

"Stick around and you might see more."

He quirked a brow. "I'm not sure I could handle it."

I laughed as his eyes gleamed mischief. "I need to deliver some shrimp and grits to Betty." I toed the ground, embarrassed about what I was going to say next. "I know we were supposed to have dinner, but I may have to help Betty some with the whole chicken judging thing, too. Want to meet up later?"

He nodded. "Maybe we can have ice cream over our cobbler."

My eyes flared. "Oh, and I'll add jelly beans to mine. Think cinnamon would be good?"

"Pepper, I think any kind you wanted to add would be good."

I tried to hide the smile that danced on my lips, but was pretty sure I fell way short. "Sounds good. Text me in a little bit."

We parted ways. I couldn't help but glance over my shoulder as he walked in the other direction. I also couldn't help but note that he glanced over his shoulder, too, and gave me a quick wave as my heart sang with happiness.

I reached Betty's booth. "I've got your shrimp and grits."

My grandmother immediately pulled me to the side. "We've got bigger problems than shrimp and grits. Melbalean's hen," she whispered, "is laying eggs like they're going out of style."

I cocked a brow. "There might be a reason for that."

"Steroids?" Betty said.

I shook my head. "No." I glanced up to make sure Melbalean wasn't watching us. I relayed what I'd heard the two women whisper, about how she had spied on Betty.

Betty worked her lower lip like only an old woman could. "I knew there was something fishy about the whole thing. Judging is in half an hour. What do you think we should do?"

I didn't know if Licky and Mint had gotten into me or what, but my biscuits were pretty burned up at the idea of my grandmother being swindled out of a victory. I licked my lips and said, "I'm going to steal those eggs, and we're going to prove they're not gold."

Betty clapped me on the shoulder. "That's my girl. I'll cause a distraction."

"What distraction?"

A slow smile crept over Betty's face. "Leave that to me."

Ten minutes later I was stroking Betty's aluminum-egg-laying hen while she was standing in front of her booth.

"Oh my goodness, my hen laid a platinum egg! And are those diamonds encrusted on the surface? Well, it sure looks to be. Heavens to Betsy and I declare! I've got me a zillion dollar egg over here!"

Heads turned and jaws dropped. A low murmur took hold over the grass lawn as witches of all sorts slowly milled over to the booth.

Betty kept it up. "That diamond's the size of my pinky!"

I stifled a laugh and glanced over to Melbalean. The old woman's face had turned a deep shade of angry pink. Her jaw was clenched tight, and her bottom lip jutted out.

"Woohoo," Betty said. "Have y'all ever seen anything like this?"

She threw me a wink. "She's laying another one," I shouted.

Folks clustered around the booth. Betty thrust out the egg we'd created. We were fairly confident a little bit of broken glass and silver in dim light would look like platinum and diamonds. At least enough to create a commotion.

"Well, I'll be," a man said.

"Look at them shine," said another woman.

All the while, Melbalean was looking angrier and angrier. I figured it was only a few more seconds before her top busted clean off.

"See how they sparkle," said another woman.

"Okay, that's it," Melbalean shouted.

I crossed my fingers as she marched out of her booth and shoved her way to the front of Betty's line. "What in tarnation is going on?

There's no way that there hen is laying anything but aluminum eggs."

Betty batted her lashes. "And how would you know that, Melbalean?"

I didn't hear the rest because I took that opportunity to sneak out of the booth and creep over to Melbalean's. Luckily, all attention was on the two old women as an age-old battle for bragging rights ensued.

I made it to the open side of Melbalean's booth and peeked in. The hen sat on a box, a stack of eggs piled up behind her. Even though it was dark, I saw at least a dozen of them. Luckily, I'd brought along a sack to stuff them in. I tossed the eggs in quickly, figuring they wouldn't break if they were made of gold, or whatever substance they were supposed to be composed of.

One of them felt a little different from the others—smooth and much cooler. I didn't have time to investigate as I laid it with the rest.

As I tossed the last one in the bag, I heard Betty's high pitched whistle. You know, the one that was supposed to give me warning.

I whirled around and came nose to nose with Melbalean Mayes.

"Just what do you think you're doing?"

Wow. I was really bad at this whole sneaking around the festival thing, wasn't I? First I got in trouble with Leona and now I was caught stealing eggs from Melbalean.

I gnawed my lip and thought fast. "Um. Nothing. I'm not doing anything. Here are your eggs."

When it got right down to it, I couldn't take them, not with Melbalean right there. I caught Betty shooting me a hard look. Apparently, my grandmother thought I should be snatching them. But of course, this whole thing was her rivalry and not mine.

A loud popping sound came from overhead. I turned to see the Cotton and Cobwebs banner spark like fireworks and then burst into flames.

Arrows of fire rained on the festival goers. Several witches started screaming. The bulb lights twinkling around the area blinked out, casting us in darkness.

The banner glowed like a red-hot ember. It fluttered and snapped like a flag on a ship at sea. Then it sailed toward the ground.

It only took half a second for the entire crowd of witches to focus their attention and magic on the disaster.

Suddenly an arm snatched me away from Melbalean.

"Come on, kid, let's go."

Betty pulled me from the booths. "Looks like your aunts' bad luck followed them."

"Why do you say that?" I said, watching as a cluster of witches fought to put out the banner, even as the fire refused to extinguish. The flames rose and crackled, snapping and flicking.

"Because that's how it is whenever you get those two around. They're mischief witches."

I frowned. "That's not what they told me. They said they were organizational witches."

She cackled. "And you believed them? Here. Hold this." My grandmother thrust something into my arms.

"What is it?"

"The bag of eggs."

My jaw dropped. "Are you kidding? Melbalean is going to know we stole it."

The lights around the festival flickered to life. We stood huddled beside the courthouse where anyone could see us holding Melbalean's eggs.

Betty pulled me into the shadows. "She's not going to know nothing."

I glared at her.

She shrugged. "Well, she might suspect but it was pitch black. That old battle-ax couldn't see who actually stole it."

I smacked my forehead. "Even though she'd just watched me throwing them into the bag?"

"We'll see."

"I'm pretty sure what I'll be seeing is the inside of jail if we don't return these."

Betty yanked the sack from me with the sort of brute strength that can only be gained from years of being an old woman trying to protect your bag from purse-snatchers. "Follow my lead and you'll be fine."

I shook my head. "Lord, if we get out of this, I promise to follow the straight and narrow from now on."

She smirked. "And how much fun is that?"

"A lot more than being terrified."

A scream rang out from the booths. "Oh no! Oh no! Police, quick!"

The banner fire was dying down as folks started flocking toward the screams.

"I wonder what happened," I said.

"Let's go find out."

"What about the eggs?"

Betty agreed. "Good point. I'll bury them."

I rolled my eyes. "Great idea."

Betty snapped her fingers and the bag flew from her hands and plopped under a mound of earth.

"Right. No one will ever see them there," I said. The area looked like a pimple about to pop. Not exactly subtle.

"That's what I thought, too."

I followed Betty to the booths. She pushed her way through the crowd. "Betty Craple coming through."

Apparently, that was enough to part the Red Sea, because the crowd shifted and exhaled, giving us room.

When we reached the center of the throng, I saw what all the fuss was about. In the place where I'd darted from Melbalean's booth lay a body—Melbalean's.

Her eyes stared silently at the sky above us. Slash marks criss-crossed her throat and chest. Women sobbed behind me. I took a step back, cowering from the sight.

Betty planted her hands on her hips and said, "Dear Lord, what happened to Melbalean?"

Someone pointed to her hen, which sat quietly in the corner. Her talons and beak were marred with blood. "It looks like her hen killed her. Melbalean Mayes was killed by a chicken."

SIX

*B*etty stepped forward. "That's the stupidest thing I've ever heard. That hen didn't kill Melbalean. It just stepped in her blood."

The crowd took a collective step away. A second later, Axel stepped into the middle of the scene.

"Everybody back. Everyone back. Let's clear the area."

A few people shot him skeptical looks. I wondered what that was about, but I did as he asked, moving away. Betty came with me.

"Hold up, you two," he said.

I grimaced. "Do you mean me?"

He nodded.

"We didn't see anything. I can go ahead and tell you that right now. I was with my grandmother on the other side of the festival when this happened."

Axel tipped his head toward Betty. A strand of wavy hair fell in his eyes. He tucked it behind an ear and said, "And what about you? Do you know anything about this?"

Betty smirked. "Yeah, cause I'm a champion switch blade killer. Carry it with me wherever I go."

AMY BOYLES

"I didn't ask for sarcasm," he said.

Betty smacked her lips. "Can't help it. It's bred in me."

Axel crossed his arms. "The police will be here any minute. Anything you want to tell me before they arrive?"

Betty glanced at me to ensure my silence. "We don't know anything, Mr. Reign."

He shot me a look. "Is that true? Because there was an awful lot of commotion coming from over here before all hell broke loose."

I cleared my throat. "My grandmother's hen started laying what looked like platinum and diamond eggs. She made a big deal about it and Melbalean came over to investigate, but that's before the banner caught on fire and distracted us."

Axel narrowed his gaze at Betty. "Is that true?"

She flicked her fingers under her chin. "Since when did you become Mr. Nosy Rosy?"

Axel shifted his weight and tapped his fingers on his hips. "Since a police officer, Todd Turnkey, was killed on your front lawn. The new chief, who's on his way here, asked me to help where I can. So that's when I became Mr. Nosy Rosy."

"Oh, I didn't know that," I said.

Betty smirked. "Your boyfriend keeping secrets from you? I wouldn't kiss him anymore. Might give you a cold sore. He could be keeping that secret from you, too."

Okay. Well if that wasn't enough to stomp on my biscuit parade, I didn't know what was.

"I don't have herpes," Axel said.

I flared out my arms. "Can we please cease and desist all of this personal conversation? Axel, we don't know anything about what happened to Melbalean. We'll be happy to attest to that when the other officers get here."

Axel glanced over his shoulder. A throng of men who looked like they had been Hugh Jackman's doubles in the movie *Van Helsing* strode across the lawn straight toward us.

Axel thumbed toward them. "Great. You can tell them now."

A tall, thin drink of a cowboy looking guy strolled up. He wore spurs on his boots and dust covered his leather chaps. He brushed off his pants.

"Just got into town from the desert. That's one heck of a ride on a skillet."

The new sheriff, or whoever he was, brushed a line of grime from the brim of his hat. His gaze followed me up and down in a way that made heat rise on my cheeks. He then turned to Axel. "Great to see you, Reign. It's been too long."

Axel shook his hand. "Good to see you, Young."

This Garrick fellow dipped his hat at us. "Garrick Young. Just flew into town." He glanced over at Melbalean's lifeless body. "Looks like I arrived at a good time."

He glanced at the row of police behind him. "Clear the scene. Get some evidence. Question folks. Let's get rolling."

A few officers threw Axel mistrustful glances, but they didn't say anything. I wondered what that was about, but shrugged it off.

Needless to say, the festivities ended for the night as people were questioned and Melbalean's body checked for prints. I watched as Melbalean's hen was whisked into a cage.

I was waiting to be released with the rest of the festival goers when that new sheriff, Garrick, strolled up to me. He shifted his lithe body onto one hip and flicked his fingers. "Axel says you talk to animals."

I brushed a strand of crimson hair from my face and nodded. "I own the familiar store in town. I can talk to them if they're willing. But they need to be willing. You can't make water out of sunshine."

"Unless there's a cloud nearby," Axel said, strolling up.

Our gazes locked and I glanced away from his smiling face. "Right. Unless that."

Garrick's gaze flickered from Axel to me. "No one here seems to know anything. That hen's my best shot at getting a solid lead. With lights out and everyone's whereabouts accounted for, the chicken's the best witness we've found."

I scoffed. "I bet you never imagined there'd be a day that you'd say that."

Garrick clicked his tongue. "You're right." He placed a hand on my back, guiding me toward the cage. He glanced over. "Reign, you coming with us?"

Axel's gaze hardened. His eyes flicked from Garrick's hand just above my waist to the hen. "Right behind you," he said stiffly.

I couldn't help but grin as we crossed to the bird. Not because Axel was jealous but because there were some things you just couldn't hide your feelings about—and liking someone was one of them.

I nearly pumped my fist in victory.

We reached the hen, who clucked at us as we approached. Garrick acknowledged me. "Go for it. Do your thing."

I cleared my throat and said, "Hey hen, I know you're probably really upset about what happened and we are, too. But we need to find out about Melbalean, the woman who was your owner. She's been hurt."

The chicken stared at me.

I sighed. I didn't think hens had enough brain to communicate with me, but before I told the brand spanking new sheriff that, I'd give it one more try.

I leaned over, getting eye level with the bird. "The lights went out a few minutes ago and we think someone attacked Melbalean at that time. Did you happen to see who did it?"

The chicken cocked one eye on me. Its comb flopped to the side as it twitched and jerked.

I sighed and glanced over my shoulder at Axel. "It's no use. I tried talking to Betty's hen earlier and didn't get anywhere with it. I hate to say it, but I don't think chicken's brains are large enough to talk to humans."

"Speak for yourself, bird brain."

The voice was distinctly high pitched and quite clipped, like the wings of a flightless bird. I slowly pivoted my head to the chicken.

"Did you say that?"

The hen fluttered its wings. "Am I the only one with brains around here? Even a worm could've figured out who spoke."

I tamped down the anger flaring in my gut. "There's no need to insult anyone."

44

"You're the one who called me stupid."

"I didn't call you stupid. I said you don't have a large enough brain to form complex speech."

"How does *Supercalifragilisticexpialidocious* do for complex speech?"

"Whoa," I said, backing up.

Axel leaned over my shoulder. His breath warmed my cheek when he spoke. "So this one talks."

I nodded. "Yes. She can do some serious talking."

Garrick strode forward. "Well? Does she know?"

My gaze flickered to him. "She hasn't said." I glanced at the hen. "So Mrs. Hen, do you happen to know what happened to Melbalean? When the lights went out, that is?"

"Of course, I know," she clucked.

I waited for her to continue, but apparently, the bird needed an invitation. "What was it you saw?"

"That old lady who kept stealing my eggs was attacked."

I curled my fingers around the wires on the cage. "Yes. Who was it? Did you see them?" The hen pecked my fingers. "Ouch!"

"Sorry. Force of habit. I see fingers, I peck."

"It's okay. Now. What did the person look like? The one who attacked Melbalean?"

The hen clucked and cooed until she finally fixed her gaze on something behind us. "There," she said. "I saw that person attack the old lady."

My head swiveled. The crowd of town folks was thicker than wet red clay. "Which one?"

The hen pecked toward the very center. "That old witch there, the one with the curly hair wearing the running shoes."

My heart weighed a ton as I zeroed in on the figure the hen was referring to. There was no way around *who* the hen had picked out.

There was only one old lady wearing running shoes—shoes that had helped us sprint across the lawn only half an hour earlier.

Axel shot me a sympathetic look as Garrick thumbed toward her. "Who's that?" he said.

Someone shouted out from behind us. "That's Betty Craple. If anyone had a reason to kill Melbalean Mayes, it was her."

SEVEN

Betty grabbed my hands as the new sheriff started leading her away for questioning. "There's a whole list of things I need you to do."

"What are you talking about?" I said.

"You think this town runs on its own elbow grease and cornbread? No. I'm the one who keeps it going. There's a list. You'll find it in my dresser. Mattie can help you."

"But you're coming back, aren't you?" I said. I glanced up at Garrick. "You're only taking her in for questioning, right?"

"You heard the hen. It saw her."

I shook my head. "I was with Betty the whole time. No way it was her. The hen didn't see things correctly. It is a chicken, after all."

Garrick dipped his head. "We'll weigh that as well. But right now we're taking her in and checking things out. Looking for evidence."

Betty shot me a pleading glance. "Get the list. Do the things. I'll be home soon. These coppers won't crack me."

"Because there's nothing to crack," I said.

Betty's bottom lip stiffened. "That, too."

As Garrick led her away, my legs weakened. I raked my fingers through my hair, knowing that Betty was innocent but there was nothing I could do about it.

A hand squeezed my shoulder. "It'll be okay."

I glanced up at Axel. I bit my lower lip. I didn't trust myself to say anything. I didn't think I would start crying over Betty being questioned by the police, but I might.

"They'll talk to her tonight, get her story, see if she has any evidence on her. If she's clean, they'll let her go."

"She was with me the whole time," I whispered. "She didn't do it."

He gave a curt nod and said, "Let me walk you home."

I grabbed Betty's hen and stowed her in a cardboard box. I followed Axel numbly through the crowd of waning festival goers. We strolled through the crowd until we reached Bubbling Cauldron Road.

He spotted the box. "Let me take that for you."

"You think they'll only keep her tonight?" I said.

Axel nodded. "They'll probably release her in a few hours. Betty Craple is pretty important to this town."

I bit back a bitter laugh. "Yeah. Apparently, she has a whole list of things she does. Keeps it in her dresser drawer. Wants me to check it out."

"Be careful. You might go blind if you see some of those things."

I did a double take. "What?"

His eyes slid until they caught my gaze. "I'm joking. There's no telling what Betty's up to. Try not to worry about her too much."

I clicked my tongue. "How can I not? That hen said she saw Betty do it. There's no way, but why did the chicken say that?"

Axel scratched his chin. "Chalk it up to bird brain?"

"Are you trying to be funny?"

He shook his head. "No. I'm serious. The hen may not have seen what she thought she did. Could've been another old lady. Heck, she could have seen Melbalean herself."

"But someone attacked Melbalean and by the time the lights came on, there wasn't one person covered in blood on the scene."

"Except the chicken," he said.

I smirked. "No way did the hen do it."

But then I remembered that Betty's own hen had attacked us earlier in the day. It was strong, but not strong enough to make one of us look like the victim in a slasher movie. It wasn't, right? Couldn't do that sort of damage.

"Betty's hen tried to peck us to death earlier," I said.

Axel quirked a brow. "Really?"

"Yeah," I said. "Something seemed to snap in it. It was strange and came out of nowhere. You think it's worth checking into?"

He adjusted his grip on the box. "If it's an option, I'll look into it. Can you get me the address where she bought it?"

"Should be on that box. I'll write it down for you when we get inside."

We reached the house. The guard-vine took a long sniff of us both but let us pass without incident. I stepped inside and there stood Amelia in her Farrah Fawcett hair and Cordelia. They sat at the table drinking coffee.

"Axel, I don't know if you've met my new cousin, Farrah," I said.

Amelia rolled her eyes. "Very funny. But we had such a good time that Lane and I are going out again tomorrow."

"You do look different," Axel said.

Amelia nodded enthusiastically. "Yeah. I've got extensions, highlights, contouring makeup—the works. I'm practically a whole new person."

Cordelia stirred sugar into her cup. "Where's Grandma?"

I shot Axel a look. "They took her in for questioning in the murder of Melbalean Mayes."

Amelia and Cordelia's jaws dropped. "What?"

I explained everything while Axel recorded the information about the hen.

"This never would've happened if our mothers hadn't returned from their trip around the world," Amelia said.

Cordelia agreed. "They bring bad luck everywhere they go. We're lucky the entire festival didn't explode."

"I don't know why anyone would give them any roles of responsibility," Amelia said. "Everyone knows they're chaos witches."

I frowned. "I thought they were mischief witches. That's what Betty said."

"What they are is up for grabs," Cordelia said lazily. "The only thing anyone can agree on is that they're trouble with a capital T."

I glanced at Axel. "You have everything you need?"

He nodded.

"I'll walk you out."

"Don't worry," Amelia said, "we're not going to tell you not to kiss —you know, like Betty would."

I closed my eyes. Her saying anything about kissing was as bad as Betty mentioning it. I gave a wave and said, "Thanks."

I followed Axel outside into the muggy night. A nearby honeysuckle vine filled the air with the sweet scent. I inhaled deeply as Axel stared up at the stars.

"It was good seeing you," he said. "It had been too long."

"Yeah."

We stared at each other. The humidity seemed to thicken—or was that simply the energy buzzing around us? Or was that just my girlie hormones doing their thing?

Probably stupid hormones.

His gaze caught mine and I sucked in a breath. I felt my lower lip tremble and I glanced away quickly, staring at the empty street.

"You found the information on the hen?" I said.

He glanced at his phone. "Stored it in here. I'll check it out tomorrow. Let you know what I find out."

"Great." I swung my fist into the opposite palm. "Well, it was great seeing you." As I felt that no kiss was coming, I might as well go inside. Besides, we'd decided we were just friends. I guess? Or at least we weren't going to get involved with each other.

I turned to go.

"Pepper."

I swung around quickly. "Yes?"

He opened his mouth, paused and said, "It was good seeing you."

I stepped forward. "You already said that."

"I'm saying it again."

I quirked a brow. "I don't believe you. I think you were going to say something else."

He rocked closer, until we were only chest width apart. "What if I was?"

"You could just say it—trust me."

"You don't know me."

"People only really get to know one another when they *know* one another."

"Half this town doesn't trust me."

"But you live here," I said. "They have to trust something about you."

"Maybe you should side with them."

"Why should I? Garrick trusts you."

He slid a hand along my arm. My skin practically popped and sizzled under his touch. "We've known each other awhile."

"And these people don't know me at all, but they've accepted me. You didn't kill anyone, did you?"

He chuckled as he brought his lips to my knuckles. "Not even close."

I stepped close enough that he had two choices—kiss me or jilt me. I was hoping he'd kiss me.

"I felt like you were going to tell me your secret," I whispered.

His gaze darkened and I immediately knew I'd said the wrong thing. Axel dropped my hand and grazed his lips over my cheek. "Good night."

My heart plummeted to the ground, going past my feet and falling until it hit the center of the earth's core, where it burst into flames.

I sighed and went inside. Amelia and Cordelia had abandoned the table and were probably in their rooms. I didn't feel like talking about what had happened that night anymore, but I needed to find out what it was Betty needed me to do.

I trudged upstairs to her room. Now, I'd never actually been invited into Betty's room before and I was a little nervous that the whole place was booby trapped. There wasn't any evidence to think this way, just a sixth sense about Betty.

Call it intuition.

Mattie sat perched outside Betty's room. "I heard about what the heck happened, sugar. What a cotton pickin' mess."

"Yeah. It is. But I'm hoping they'll figure it out quickly."

Mattie rubbed her side against my leg. "I'm guessin' from the fact that you're headin' for Betty's room that she told you about The List."

My eyebrows lifted. "You know about it?"

Mattie meowed softly. "Know about? I'm the one who helped her write it."

"Impressive." I started to push on the door and stopped. "I'm not going to blow up if I walk through there, am I?"

"Shoot no," Mattie said. "Come on. I'll show you where it is."

"I hope it's not too long," I grumbled.

I followed Mattie as she padded into the room. For all of Betty's shotgun-toting ways, her room was surprisingly sweet and simple, feeling more like a room at a B&B than a kitchen witch's chamber.

Lace doilies sprinkled the surfaces and a beautiful blue quilt covered her four-poster bed. The furniture was cherry with a rocker tucked into the corner.

Mattie jumped silently onto the chest of drawers. "List is in the top one. Should be laminated."

Laminated?

I eased open the drawer and peered inside. Rows of neatly folded clean white underwear sat on one side while columns of white socks sat on the other.

"It's under the underwear," Mattie said.

"Great."

Mattie half purred half laughed. "Betty figured no one wanted to dig through her underwear to find that list."

"She'd be right."

"But it's highly important. This town don't run right if all those boxes ain't checked. With her out of commission, it's up to you to lead this town so it don't fall apart."

"No pressure." I took a deep breath and plunged my hand under the mountain of old lady Hanes. My fingers slid across the bottom until they felt the edge of the laminated sheet. I pulled it out and started reading.

"Every morning, you've got to find Peter Potion, put clothes on him and get him home." I jerked back. "I'm sorry. What?"

Mattie sighed. "Peter Potion is the mayor. He's been mayor for a good ten years. He's also the town drunk, but no one knows it."

I poked the sheet. "Clearly someone does."

Mattie blinked her green eyes at me. "You're right, Betty knows, but she's tried hard to keep his reputation. He don't drink on the job, only at night at home. But he gets so drunk he sleepwalks through the town. Naked."

My eyes flared. "Naked?"

Mattie rubbed a paw over her whiskers. "You got that right. And every morning he winds up in a public place. So every day Betty tracks him down, puts clothes on him and gets him to bed."

I shook my head, not believing what I was hearing. "Why? Why not let him get found and humiliated enough so he stops drinking?"

Mattie curled her tail around her legs. "She don't want to hurt his feelings."

I stared at her. "Betty Craple, the woman who supposedly put this whole town to sleep so she could streak naked through it, gets up every morning at the butt crack of dawn, tracks down Peter Potion and tucks him into bed?"

"You got it. She sets out about four am."

I cringed. "Okay. Well, what about the other things on this list?"

Mattie jumped into the drawer, landing on the socks. "The Conjuring Caverns only have to be cleaned out once a week, and Betty did it this morning, so you're safe until next Saturday, and the last thing will need to be done in two nights, but Betty should be back by then."

My gaze skimmed until I read the very last line. "There's nothing on the last line, but it happens in two nights?"

Mattie nodded. "That's on a need to know basis."

An inkling of an idea tickled my brain. I wasn't sure if I was right, but when I'd first arrived into town, on the last full moon, I'd gone on a moonlit cast iron skillet ride with half of the town. I'd ended up plummeting into the Cobweb Forest and found myself face to face with a chained werewolf.

Betty had been standing guard over him, a shotgun in her hands. I never found out the details about who the werewolf was, because Betty didn't mention it again. I felt like it was some big, dark secret that Magnolia Cove gripped with steel talons.

"Don't worry, sugar," Mattie said. "You won't have to do the last line."

"Is it the werewolf?" I said.

"Need to know basis," Mattie reminded me.

I cracked the knuckles of my right hand. "And what if she's not back?"

Mattie yawned. "Then you'll need to know. We'll worry if that happens. Now get to bed, you need some rest if you're going to wake up and catch old Peter."

I nodded. Naked mayors, secrets and cleaning the Conjuring Caverns. I sure hoped Betty came home soon, because it looked like I had my work cut out for me.

"Oh, and Pepper," Mattie called as I was about to slink out the door.

"Yes?"

"Sometimes Peter likes to put up a fight."

Great.

EIGHT

$\mathcal{J}$ sneaked out of the house at exactly four am, a to-go cup of coffee in one hand and a pack of jelly beans in the other. Sugar and caffeine were my two best friends.

Before I left, Mattie told me all of Peter's favorite haunts—or places to crash in the buff, as I liked to think of them.

Unfortunately, Mattie had decided not to come with me, but she suggested I bring a blanket to cover the good mayor.

I brought an extra-wide wool cover that didn't even let one glimmer of light pass through. I'd also contemplated telling Cordelia and Amelia what I was up to, but Mattie had warned me against it. According to the cat, if Betty had wanted them to know, she would've told them.

So here I was, stalking around Magnolia Cove before dawn looking like a Peeping Tom. Luckily, Peter's favorite spots to crash were all within about five minutes of each other, so I should have things wrapped up pretty quickly.

The first spot, the bench in front of the courthouse, was bare, so I checked it off the list. I walked on to the second spot, which was a weird one, but I supposed I could understand it.

In the center of the town square stood a concrete statue of one of the founding witches of Magnolia Cove—an Amaryllis Snitch. Amaryllis was posed squatting with her arms out. Apparently, the mayor liked to curl up in her statue.

Weird but true.

When I found Amaryllis's arms empty, I took a right and headed to the candy store. Apparently, Peter sometimes unlocked my cousin Carmen's shop and holed up with stacks of chocolate and lollipops.

Sure enough, I received a spectacular view of Peter's backside from the store's front. The mayor had decided to snooze in the window.

Awesome.

Time to be quick. The door was unlocked. The bell tinkled when I entered. Peter shuffled a bit, turning away from me.

His large beer belly spread nearly to his chin. I held the blanket in front of me and draped it over his hairy body.

Peter grumbled as he pivoted. "Sorry, Betty. Had to have a caramel frog cluster."

"No problem, Pete," I said, going along with it.

He blinked several times until he focused a hazy gaze on me. "You're not Betty."

I tucked the blanket around him and said, "I'm her granddaughter, Pepper. Betty's busy this morning."

A stale breath wheezed from his mouth. I stopped inhaling to spare myself the breath of death. "We're expecting her home tomorrow," I said. "Now, let's get you up before the town wakes and sees you."

I helped Peter sit and finished draping the blanket around both his sides as he heaved and rose.

I escorted him from the shop. "How'd you get in?"

Peter pointed to a ceramic spider just outside the door. "Key's in there."

I found the key under one of the spindly legs and locked the door. "Come on, show me where you live."

Light was beginning to bloom over the horizon when we reached the mayor's yellow cottage. Lace curtains hung in the windows. It was completely different from what I expected.

"Pretty cottage," I said.

"My wife picked it out."

"Your wife?" I said. *Shouldn't she be the one saving you every morning?*

"She passed away not long ago."

"Oh," I said quietly. "I'm sorry."

We walked in and the mayor disappeared into a back room. "Pepper," he called out, sounding much more alert than he had when I'd first woken him, "I can't tell you how ashamed I am of my behavior."

"It's all right," I said.

"It's not, though. I've been mayor for ten years and if it weren't for your grandmother, most of the town would know my secret. If she didn't make it a priority to find me every morning and get me home, my reputation would be ruined."

"I understand," I said.

"Where is she, anyway?"

I sighed. "Melbalean Mayes was murdered at the festival last night."

The mayor reappeared dressed in a robe. The scent of cologne wafted off him. I had to admit, it was much better smelling than stale beer breath.

He pulled a toothbrush from behind him and started on his teeth. He spoke between scrubs. "Well, that was bound to happen. She might've had a lot of folks fooled, but Melbalean was no saint. You could look at her son and know that's the truth."

I crossed my arms and leaned on one hip. "Problem is, Betty looks guilty. They had that stupid rivalry about the best creature."

Peter spit into the sink. "Yeah. That's been going on for years. But the rumors swirling around Melbalean was that she would take things from people."

I took a risk and sat in his recliner. Taking a risk because I had no idea how many times Peter's naked rear end had graced it. It didn't look crusty or smell bad, so that was certainly a plus.

"What things did she take?" I said.

Peter grabbed a bottle of mouthwash that he kept by his kitchen sink. Listen, who am I to judge? But anyway, he took a swig, gargled for about half a minute and then spit into the basin. He flattened his gray-streaked hair with his palm.

"She'd take whatever you were willing to sell—that was the rumor, at least. I never wanted to get rid of anything. I'm a wizard so there isn't much I can't do. But a less powerful witch who wanted to attract a certain man, she might be drawn to what Melbalean could do for her."

I dusted dirt off my pants. "I'm new to this whole witch business, and at the most, I can talk to animals and occasionally use my power when I'm in danger. So you'll have to spell it out for me—what exactly would Melbalean do for someone?"

Peter opened his fridge, pulled out an apple and chomped into it. "Say you were a witch and you wanted to win a dance competition. If you went to Melbalean she would ensure that you won—but the price would be hefty."

"What price would you pay?"

He chewed for a moment. "There was a rumor years ago this exact thing happened to a beautiful young woman—she wanted to win a dance contest, but she could sing, too. Another one of her prized possessions. Well, to win the dance, the witch gave Melbalean her voice."

My jaw dropped. "Her voice? Like in *The Little Mermaid*?"

"Just like that. Now, Melbalean wasn't stupid. She didn't poop where she ate."

Realization hit me like water off a semi-truck going full speed down the highway during a rainstorm. "So she didn't practice this sort of magic around here."

"Not on the locals, no," Peter said. "But rumors don't start for no reason and Rufus didn't become Dr. Zhivago on his own."

"I think you mean Frankenstein."

"Hmm?" he said between bites.

"Frankenstein. Not Zhivago. Zhivago was a guy in Russia."

Mayor Potion nodded emphatically. "Yes, I think you're right.

Anyway. What I'm saying is, Melbalean probably had worse enemies than Betty Craple."

"Not according to her hen. The bird told me that Betty did it."

Peter shrugged. "This new sheriff, I think he'll be smart enough to discount the ramblings of a birdbrain."

I grimaced. "I sure do hope so."

Peter wiped a pudgy hand along his face. "I agree. I'm used to Betty seeing me in the buff every morning, but you were quite the surprise." His gaze dashed around the room nervously. "You're not, um, going to mention this to anyone, are you?"

I hid the smile that crept across my face. "Don't worry, Mayor, your secret is safe with me."

THE TREK to the house left my mind spinning. If Melbalean had been as horrible as they said, surely there would be some evidence of that in her home.

Wouldn't there be?

I was deep in thought and wasn't watching where I was walking when a voice called out. "You going to look up or bump right into me?"

I jerked back, clutching my chest. "Sorry." My gaze snagged on Axel dressed in sweatpants, a t-shirt and running shoes. "Are you running?"

He laughed. "Don't look so surprised. I have to work for this body, you know."

"I figured it came naturally to you."

He shook his head. "You want to come along?"

I glanced down. I was basically dressed for a jog. What the heck? "Sure." I realized I could use his opinion. "In fact, I need your help."

He stopped. Took a deep breath and swiped a line of sweat from his forehead. "Come on. Normally I don't like to think when I run, but I'll make an exception."

"Great," I said.

AMY BOYLES

The tension from the night before had vanished between us, which I took to be a solid sign that we were on the right road with our friendship, or whatever it was.

"Mind me asking what you're doing up and about so early," he said.

I opened my mouth and then clamped it shut quickly. "If I told you, I'd have to kill you."

He kicked up a jog and I ran beside him. "I'm guessing it has something to do with Betty."

"That's as much as I'll say."

"Just don't get arrested," he said.

I sucked air. "About that."

"Not a good way to start a conversation," he said.

"Anyway. From what I understand, Melbalean might not've been what she seemed."

"I've heard the rumors."

I paused, trying to think of a good way to explain the situation, when he kicked up the pace. I sprinted forward. "Listen, if she was into something bad, do you think there'd be evidence in her house?"

"Probably. But that's not my concern."

Hmm. Obviously, I wouldn't be able to talk him into breaking and entering this morning. "Do you think maybe someone was getting revenge on her? Planned the whole thing at the festival?"

"I think that's the most obvious part of the whole situation."

"Is there any way to know who rigged the lights to flicker out and the banner to explode?"

Axel shook his head. "Not that I'm aware of." He stopped, panting. "Listen, I know you want to help, but Betty'll probably be released today."

I frowned. "What if she's not?"

"She didn't have any blood on her and you were with her. My guess is the forensic evidence is slim."

I found it funny that witches would use forensics and not magic. "They test for those kinds of things? Hair and stuff?"

Axel picked up speed again. "Yeah. They don't just use voodoo and pixie dust to solve crimes."

60

"Oh? Can you use those things, too?"

Axel shot me a questioning glance. I widened my eyes and put on a goofy look so that he'd know I was joking.

"We also use snips and snails and puppy dogs' tails," he joked.

"And don't forget sugar and spice and all things nice," I said.

We slowed to cross a street. "What about Melbalean's family? Does she have a husband?"

"He died years ago," Axel said. "She lived alone."

Score! So if I had to break into her house for any reason, I'd be able to.

"Why do you ask?"

"No reason," I said.

Axel's watch blipped a message. I didn't see what it was, but after he read it, Axel's blue eyes darkened to a turbulent sea and his jaw clenched.

"What is it?"

"You know Melbalean will be having a funeral soon—in a couple of days. That's how witches do it."

"Why only two days?"

Axel shrugged. "The story was that if you didn't bury a witch quickly the body would burn up, evaporate into the air. Comes from the times when everyone thought witches were evil."

"That's nice," I said sarcastically.

"I don't make the rules, I only relay them. Anyway, that's the way it goes. She'll be buried tomorrow."

"Why does it matter?" I said.

Axel stopped, inhaled a deep shot of air. Sweat sprinkled his brow and dripped down the slope of his nose. "I'm telling you this because I want you to be prepared."

"For what?" I said.

"For Rufus."

A cold chill swept my body at the mention of Rufus.

I swallowed a knot in my throat. "What do you mean?"

Axel's jaw flexed when he said, "He's coming for the funeral."

NINE

"*B*ut I thought he couldn't come into Magnolia Cove?" I said. We were walking now. All my steam had vanished as soon as the name Rufus had been mentioned.

Axel placed a comforting hand on my arm. "He can't. Not normally. But with his mother's death, the police will lift the ban on him, if the town council agrees. As long as Rufus is supervised, he'll be able to return to Magnolia Cove for the day."

I inhaled deeply, trying to tamp down the geyser of panic thrusting its way up my throat. "So what should I do?"

Axel shook his head. "There's nothing for you to do. I'll keep you posted on the situation and don't worry, I'll follow Rufus, make sure he doesn't try anything."

I nodded quietly.

Axel took me in his arms and wrapped me in an unexpected hug. My hands hung numbly from my sides, but only for half a second before I realized I'd get to feel his muscular body beneath my palms if I reacted fast enough.

I reacted fast enough.

I contemplated bursting into tears 'cause then I'd really get a lot more hugs, but I stopped myself. I was a business owner and a responsible person.

Though I had to admit, I liked having his arms around me.

Axel whispered in my ear. "I won't let anything happen to you."

I pulled away and nodded. "Thanks. But maybe Rufus won't bother me. Maybe he'll come for his mother's funeral and he won't start throwing that blue light at me and demanding I go with him or die. I mean, it could happen."

Axel grabbed my hand. "Come on, let's get you home."

We walked in silence the rest of the way. Axel dropped me off at my house. "I'll keep you posted as to what's going on."

"Thanks."

He gave me a quick hug and I walked inside. Cordelia and Amelia were up fixing a breakfast of cereal and milk.

"It's not Betty's breakfast," Cordelia said, "but we won't starve, either."

I laughed. "That's true. So she hasn't come home yet, I take it."

Amelia shook her head of extensions. "No, but it's early. Maybe they'll release her by lunch." She tapped a finger on the table. "You don't think they're interrogating her really hard, do you?"

Cordelia grimaced. "I sure hope not. She's old and ornery, but she's not a criminal."

I sank into a chair, grabbed a bowl and started building my own breakfast. "I hope they see it that way. They *are* taking the word of a bird over hers."

Amelia's eyes widened. "Oh. Yeah. Well. That's probably not so good."

I shook my head. "No, but what can we do? We have to wait for them to release her."

A loud cluck came from the cardboard box against the wall.

Cordelia frowned. "Speaking of birds, what are we going to do about that one?"

I smirked. "I need to feed the animals. I'll take the hen with me and get her out for a bit."

Amelia picked at her long hair. "I've got to wash it this morning for my date with Lane. I hope I can style it right and do my makeup."

Cordelia rolled her eyes. "I'll help you glam up. Don't worry."

"I know, but I have no idea how I'm going to keep doing this. I can't imitate Betty's talents. The hair is one thing—blowing it dry and styling, but the makeup—there's the highlighting and contouring. I don't know if I can do it right. What if Lane takes one look at me and wonders if I'm the same person from the night before? What if he doesn't recognize me?"

I stifled a laugh. "I think you'll be fine. If this guy doesn't like you for who you are, then he's an idiot."

Cordelia nodded. "That's exactly right."

We ate breakfast then I showered and dressed while Mattie rested on the window seat. My bedroom had been my mom's when she was growing up and according to Betty still had all the same furnishings.

The room filled me with warmth. The bright colors, the awards Mom had won—all of it made me feel close to the woman who'd died giving birth to me.

For the first time in my life, I felt like I had an inkling of who my mother had been.

Living here made me feel close to her.

"How'd it go this morning, sugar?" Mattie said.

"Fine. Peter was easy, though he mentioned something about Melbalean not being who she said she was."

Mattie blinked at me. "I tend to stay more in the animal world than the human one since I'm an animal, and that's not somethin' I'd ever heard before."

A thought occurred to me. "Did Melbalean have any pets?"

"I wouldn't know, but one of the other cats in town might."

My eyes flared with interest. "I don't know if I'll need you to ask around, but if the police don't release Betty…"

Mattie stretched. "How about I go ahead and see what I can find out? Just in case."

I sighed, relieved. "That would be great. Thank you."

"If you could just open the window for me."

I clicked my tongue. "You got it, sugarbear."

Mattie made what sounded like a cat laugh. She jumped onto the sill and padded down the side of the roof like a cat who took ballet every day of her life.

"Be careful," I said before closing the window. I washed my hands and grabbed my things, readying to head to Familiar Place and feed the critters there.

As soon as I unlocked the door and stepped inside, the animals started meowing and barking. When I wasn't at the pet shop the animals went into stasis, basically a deep slumber until I returned. It happened as soon as I closed the door and left.

I didn't know exactly how it worked, and no one else could tell me. Unfortunately, my late Uncle Donovan—Betty's brother--who'd left me the store, had died quickly from sickness and didn't leave a manual, so I pretty much had to wing the shop business.

I placed the cardboard box on the ground, pulled out the hen and placed her feed in the corner. As soon as I rose, I noticed a twinge of a headache looming behind my eyes.

Probably eye strain or something. I'd find some ibuprofen when I left and see if that took care of it.

"You brought her back," one of the kittens said.

"Can we eat her?" one of the puppies added.

I fisted my hands on my hips. "No eating the hen. She's here to walk around and get some exercise."

Most of the animals in the cages were young, hadn't lived very long. The birds were older, with I suspected more life experience, so they might have an inkling of an answer to the question I wanted to ask.

"Have any of y'all ever seen a hen attack a person and kill them?"

The animals all stopped. They stared blankly at me as if my words didn't make any sense to them.

"No," squawked one of the parrots. "I've never known that to happen."

"Hmm, that's what I was thinking."

Not that I thought that Melbalean's hen had killed her, but the animal was covered in blood and had pointed the finger at Betty.

And wouldn't that be just about perfect? A killer hen. No one would suspect it. But that still meant that someone had to cast a spell on it, or breed it for that purpose.

I sighed. Or maybe I was simply crazy with an overactive imagination. Yep. That was probably it.

Maybe Axel would find something out when he contacted the chicken seller.

A knock came from the door. I glanced up to see Cordelia tapping on the glass. I smiled and let her in.

"Hey, everything okay?"

She nodded. "Yeah. I just thought I'd come keep you company for a few minutes." She hopped onto a stool behind the cash register. "Amelia's ready for her date. She was driving me crazy, trying to figure out the perfect outfit to wear."

"I guess she likes him."

Cordelia shot me a long glance. I couldn't help but giggle at the sarcasm I sensed in the look. "She only just met him. It's not like it's love or anything."

"You never know," I said.

She shrugged. "I guess not. But the fact that our grandmother set her up would be enough to make me run for the hills."

"Maybe Betty finally got it right."

Cordelia raked her fingers through her long blond tresses. "Right and I'm betting if she were around, Betty wouldn't be waiting up for them with a shotgun tossed over her knees."

I laughed, remembering my strict ten pm curfew. If I'm not home by then, Betty's waiting behind the front door with her shotgun.

Yep. She's quite the character, my grandmother.

"That's because she only just met you," Cordelia said. "I think she worries about you more than us because you don't know much about our world. Probably why she always tells you to stop kissing, too."

"So it's because she loves me?"

Cordelia clicked her tongue. "You got it."

"What about your boyfriend, Zach?" I said.

Cordelia hugged her arms. "He's supposed to be home soon. Right now, he's looking for a lost magical civilization in the Andes."

"Wow," I said. "Impressive."

"Yeah. It's some part of our witch history he wants to recover," she said.

A dark figure suddenly fluttered in front of the door. I glanced up to see Officer Garrick Young turning the knob.

He strode in, all six foot five of him. Or however tall he was, cause this guy was tall and lean. Cordelia's eyes widened when she set eyes on him. I couldn't help but notice that Garrick flashed her a smile and held her gaze for a moment.

He shuffled in his cowboy boots. "Ladies, I'm sorry to bother you."

I stepped forward. "It's fine. My cousin Cordelia and I have been worried sick about Betty."

He tipped his hat. "Cordelia. I'm Garrick."

Red dots spotted her cheeks. "How do you do?"

"Mighty fine," he said.

Looked like those two were about to lose themselves in each other's eyes. I cleared my throat. "Is Betty okay?"

"She's doing well. But that's not why I came."

I frowned. "Why'd you come?"

He glanced at the hen strutting back and forth. "I need that bird."

"But this is Betty's hen," I said. "She doesn't know anything. Didn't see anything that I know of. I mean, I didn't try asking her about it because the last time I talked to the bird, she didn't answer. So you see, I don't think she can talk. In fact, I'd tried asking her questions before and she didn't answer. That's why I didn't think the other bird would speak, Melbalean's bird."

They both stared at me with glazed eyes. I smiled sheepishly. "Sorry. I chatter when I get nervous."

"That's quite all right," Garrick said. "I see that a lot in my business."

The implication of his words hit me. "Oh, well, I'm not nervous because I'm guilty or anything. Sometimes I just get nervous."

He slid two fingers along the brim of his hat. "That's fine, but I still need to confiscate that hen from you ladies."

"Why?" Cordelia said.

His gaze slid toward her. "Regardless of what you think, according to Betty, that hen is very important."

"How so?" I said.

Garrick's dark eyes peeked out from under the brim of his hat. "According to Betty, that bird holds the secret to who killed Melbalean."

TEN

"Oh, I just said that so they'd let me go."

Cordelia and I had returned to the house. Betty stood at the hearth. She plucked some of the herbs from the dried stalks over the mantel. She ground them between her hands and dropped them in a bubbling cauldron.

Betty snorted. "I told them to test that chicken's DNA, see if it could lead them to the killer."

I rocked in one of the chairs situated around the fireplace. "How does that help you?"

Betty grinned like an evil Disney villain. "I don't know, but I'm out, so it worked."

I sighed. *Right.* I'm sure it was all because of the chicken. "So they couldn't hold you?"

She pulled out her pipe and snapped her fingers. The end smoked as she brought it to her lips. "Didn't have any evidence that pointed to me. At least, not that I know of. But they told me not to go far, so I think they still suspect me."

I frowned. "Axel is tracking down information on the hen. Maybe that'll help us figure some things out."

Betty took a long drag of the pipe and exhaled, creating perfect smoke rings that buoyed in the air before warping into wisps. "Maybe he'll turn up something." Her gaze slid over to Amelia. "How'd things go with that boy of yours?"

Amelia smiled brightly. "Great. He's coming by soon. We'll be going out again."

Betty rubbed her hands together. "What are we doing sitting around here for, girls? We need to get lunch cracking."

In less than half a second, turnip greens boiled in the cauldron and a pan of chicken fried steak sizzled in a skillet beside it.

"Extra Crisco, if you please," I said.

"Coming right up," Betty said.

Amelia popped up beside us. "Here's the thing. I can't quite get my hair and makeup right."

A glint of mischief shone in Betty's eyes. "Leave it to me, kid."

She placed her thumb on her nose. Magic shimmered from her left nostril like sparks of fire. They danced over to Amelia, where they petered out like dying embers.

"Hmm," Betty said. "That wasn't supposed to happen."

I twisted a strand of honey and crimson hair. "You mean the part where a booger of magic blew out of your nose or the part where you snotted on her?"

Betty rested the spatula on her hip. "Very funny. I don't know what kind of manners you learned while you were living out in the wilds of America, but here in Magnolia Cove we don't talk to our elder witches like that."

I threw my arms around Betty and said, "I missed you."

She sniffled. "I missed you, too. But watch it."

"Does my hair look better?" Amelia said.

Truth be told, I hadn't noticed much difference in Amelia's hair until she raked her fingers through it and one of the tendrils fell out.

Cordelia grimaced. "I tried to help her with it earlier, but my magic isn't as good as yours," she said to Betty.

Betty huffed. "I think those police did something to me."

I picked up the strand of golden hair and handed it to Amelia. "What would they have done?"

She flicked her fingers at the food. It vanished from the hearth and reappeared on the dining table. "I told those idiots I wasn't a flight risk. Told them they didn't need to worry about me leaving town. Heck-in-high-heels, this town would explode without me."

"I think you mean implode," Cordelia said. "You know, like it would fall apart. Not blow up."

"I know what I said," Betty snapped. "And if I said explode into a million pieces of confetti, then that's what I meant."

Cordelia made an *o* with her mouth. "All right then."

"I think to keep me from leaving, they screwed with my ability to change things and create glamours. Just wait until I get my hands on that new sheriff's neck. I'm going to throttle him like a hen that's about to be Sunday dinner."

"He's kinda cute," Cordelia said shyly.

Betty's eyes sparked interest, but they quickly died when a knock came from the door.

Amelia wrung her hands. "It's him. Lane. He's here. Help. You've got to make me beautiful."

Cordelia snapped her fingers and a band appeared in her hands. "Come on. We'll give you a sloppy bun. It'll look great."

"Please don't let more hair fall out," Amelia prayed.

"If it does we'll say you've got leprosy," Betty said.

Amelia cringed. "That's horrible."

I shrugged. "Could be worse. Come on. Let's get you to the bathroom and Betty can answer the door."

Five minutes of primping and updoing Amelia's hair had her looking like a Southern prom queen and made her shine like a diamond.

"You look beautiful," I said. "Like, you could win Miss Cotton and Cobwebs."

"You think so?" she said. "I'd love to win. That is, if they keep the festival open."

"Maybe they will," I said.

We burst out of the bathroom and found Betty stuffing Lane full of sweet tea and cheese biscuits.

Lane's gaze swept across the room and landed on Amelia. "How is it you can look more beautiful than you did yesterday?"

Wow. I wasn't sure whether to throw up or be really impressed with him.

"Lane, you're so sweet," Amelia said. "Would you like to join us for lunch?"

He nodded. "I'd love to."

Betty dished up everyone's plates and we'd just sat when another knock came from the door.

"I'm not expecting anyone," Cordelia said.

"Me, neither," I said.

Betty nodded to Amelia, who scooted from her seat and crossed the living room. I heard the door open and slam just as quickly.

"No one was there," Amelia said.

She moved toward us when the knocking started again.

"Well somebody's there," Betty said.

"Nope. No one. Just a magical practical joke," Amelia insisted.

The rapping loudened until Betty threw her napkin on the table and crossed to the door. Amelia curled a hand around her arm. "I promise. It's no one."

"No one who knocks like a bear? You can bet your biscuits I'm not that stupid." She threw open the door.

In walked Licky and Mint.

No wonder Amelia had pretended no one was here. Licky, Amelia's mother, took one look at her daughter and said, "Why Amelia, I almost didn't recognize you. What have you done to your hair?"

Amelia smiled brightly as Lane focused his attention on her. "Oh, you know, it's just some hairspray and a little teasing. Nothing serious."

Mint pulled up a chair. "Sunday dinner at Mama's. There ain't nothing like this in all the world." She grabbed a square of fried meat, dragged it through a dish of white gravy and took a bite. "Umm-hmm. Nothing like it."

Betty pointed a finger at her. "Y'all two had better not call down a flock of pooping seagulls onto my house. Or anything else. We're trying to enjoy a nice meal with Amelia's new boyfriend, Lane."

Lane choked. "Boyfriend?"

Amelia intervened quickly. "We've only just met. Lane's not exactly my boyfriend. Not that he couldn't be," she said quickly. "But as of right now, he isn't."

"That's good," Licky said. "Take it slow. Let him know all your quirks. Like the fact that you used to pick your nose and eat your boogers when you were little."

Amelia's eyes widened to saucers.

Mint picked up where Licky dropped off. "Or the fact that when she was little, you could light Amelia's farts and power all of Magnolia Cove with them."

Amelia's head fell into her hands.

Lane smiled widely. "I think my mom would've said the same thing about me."

Amelia raised her face so we could see her, but from her expression, I could tell she wasn't sure whether to be relieved or horrified.

"But no matter what," Mint said, poking the air with the steak, "the most interesting thing Amelia's done is to change from that pixie cut to this look. And she's even wearing makeup."

Amelia rose. "Okay. That's great. Wow. I think the festival committee is calling for you. I hear the loudspeaker through the walls."

"I don't hear it," Licky said.

"Well, I do," Amelia said.

"Me, too," I seconded, trying to help out my cousin.

"Oh yes," Cordelia added. "I think Mayor Potion is talking now. You'd better get over there to see what all the fuss is about."

I rose and gently started pushing Licky toward the door. "Yes, time to go."

She turned toward Amelia. "Well, okay. But we wanted to stop by." She paused and squinted. "Amelia, what's that hanging from your ear?"

Amelia clutched the top of her lobe. "Nothing. Not a thing."

But I could see a blond tendril of hair had fallen. I glanced worriedly at her makeup. The contouring job we'd done was unraveling quickly, and her features were returning to their normal pixie look instead of the lush, Farrah Fawcett thing she had going on.

Betty rose. "Lane, it looks like we're having a little family craziness right now." She clapped her hands and a to-go container appeared, chock full of food. "Can you call on Amelia later? That is, if you don't have to scale a mountain."

Lane flashed his thousand-watt smile and said, "I'm not scaling mountains for a couple of days. I can come back. I see there's a lot going on."

He gave Amelia a quick wave and headed out the door, squeezing between Licky and Mint, who weren't going anywhere fast.

As soon as he was gone, Amelia spewed a well of anger toward her mother and aunt.

"Do you two intentionally go around wrecking people's lives? Who tells their daughter's boyfriend that she used to eat boogers? And what aunt talks about flatulence?"

The walls practically shook from her anger. I cringed, wedging my back into the wall.

"We're sorry, dear," Licky said.

"Get out! Just get out. I don't want to see you ever again!"

The room stilled to an eerie silence. Mint and Licky exchanged a look. It was Mint who spoke. "Let's go."

They left quietly. As soon as they were gone, Betty turned to Amelia. "Don't stress yourself out, dear. It'll make your hair fall out."

As if on cue, the entire head of fake hair that Amelia wore detached from her scalp and plopped in a heap on the floor.

Amelia screamed and ran upstairs.

Betty smiled at us. "Don't worry, I'll make Lane go bald overnight so that they match."

ELEVEN

$\mathcal{M}$y head was still pounding. Imagine after that fiasco of a Sunday meal, I had a headache. I'm sure you're surprised.

But anyway, I took a nap, and was awakened to the sound of scratching. I blinked my eyes open and saw Mattie pawing at the window.

Groggy with a brain full of fuzz, I teetered over and opened it.

"Sugar, I been tappin' for five minutes. You were out cold."

I yawned. "Yeah. I'm a little tired. Come on in."

She padded from the window seat onto my bed and started licking her paws. Here I was waiting for her to give me some serious intel, and she was taking a bath.

"So did you find anything out?" I said.

Mattie stopped, blinked at me. "Oh sugar, yes. Sorry, I got cat brain."

I straightened the sheets and pillows on the bed. "Is that like a short-term memory problem?"

Mattie nodded. "Kinda. My brain ain't big like yours, so I forget."

The way she looked at me, I wasn't sure if she was calling my big brain a plus or a minus. To be honest, it didn't matter to me.

"Okay, what'd you find out?"

Mattie stopped licking herself. "I met this mouse who claims that inside the house are all sorts of strange things."

"Really?"

Mattie meowed. "That's what he said."

"Did you go in?"

She shook her head. "No. But we're meeting the mouse there tonight."

"We are?"

"Yep. As soon as it gets dark, we'll head on over."

"Okay, great." I cringed.

"What's wrong?"

I rubbed my temples. "I've got this headache that won't go away."

"Sugar, did you forget that if you don't use your powers, they build up? That buildup can give you a headache."

I grimaced. "Yeah, I guess with everything that's going on I forgot."

"You need to use up some magic. Why don't we go ahead and get ready? By the time we work on your power, it'll be time to meet the mouse at Melbalean's."

"Sounds like a plan."

I packed a knapsack with a flashlight, water and snacks in case I got hungry. A short time later we were ready to head from the house.

I noticed Betty rocking beside the fire. "You okay?"

She grabbed her middle. "I'm not feeling well. I think those idiot police did something to me."

"You look a little pale. Are you sure you're not catching a cold?"

Betty shook her head. "I don't get sick. Ever. I'm immune."

I clicked my tongue. "From sickness."

"Right." She paused. Her glassy eyes roamed the room. Yep. She looked kinda sick to me, but what did I know? "If I need you to, can you do the morning grab-and-go of Pete?"

I nodded. "Sure."

Mattie and I left, cutting through the Cotton and Cobwebs festival. There were plenty of people in attendance, but the energy from yesterday had waned.

A whiff of grilled meat drifted up my nostrils, making my stomach rumble. I glanced around to see where it was coming from and saw another line at Leona's, though Leona wasn't the person dishing up food.

My gaze drifted to the booths where Betty and Melbalean had set up shop. Yellow "Do Not Cross" tape hung limply around the structure, and a tarp draped the one where Melbalean had been murdered.

A figure shuffled out from behind the booths. It was Leona. She was scurrying around as if looking for something.

"What's she doing there?" I said.

"Probably looking for a raccoon to cook up," Mattie said.

I stared at her. "You're kidding, right?"

Mattie meowed. "'Course. Everybody knows Leona don't cook up raccoon."

"That's good."

"She prefers possum."

"That does not make me feel better."

Mattie padded forward. "I was kidding, sugar. Come on. Let's go see if we can find a quiet spot to work your magic."

"Where are we going exactly?"

Mattie's green eyes flashed as she glanced at me. "Why, the Conjuring Caverns, of course. They're full of magic and things that might scare you."

"Like what?"

"Spiders."

"Yep, that'll work," I said.

I was not crazy about spiders. I followed Mattie across town to a grassy knoll with a hole in it. Water dripped from the opening, and a grate covered the bottom. "This looks like a sewer."

Mattie laughed. "It's the low part of the caves. Just trust me. You enter on one end and wind up in another."

I edged back. "Say what?"

Mattie flicked her tail as she pranced forward. "That's how it works. Come on."

I dipped my head to avoid colliding with what looked like wet seaweed. The smell of mildew drifted up my nostrils. I touched a wall and layer of slime attached to my palm.

Gross.

This was more like something out of a Stephen King novel than what I'd consider Conjuring Caverns. But luckily, the hole opened after a few feet, becoming a brown cave. Light from outside dappled the walls until we were far enough back that the cavern darkened.

Fear of dark, tight places constricted my throat. "How far are we supposed to go?"

"We're almost there."

A few more hesitant steps in and light burst forth. I was suddenly facing the opposite direction, as if I were leaving the sewer. Because no matter what way you spun it, we were in a sewer.

Water dripped from the ceiling into a small pool that seemed lit from within. Crystalline water glowed. The scent of mildew had vanished, and in its place was the sharp smell of pine trees.

"Where are we?" I said.

"On the other side of Magnolia Cove. It's a shortcut, but it will also work with trying to get rid of your magic."

I quirked a brow at her. "How is this going to help?"

Mattie crept around to one side of the puddle and sat. "That water holds things you're afraid of. That's why this place is called Conjuring Caverns. There's a lot of power here. But what that there pool will do is show your fears. I figure we throw somethin' scary enough at you, you'll use a burst of power."

"Oh."

She was probably right. Every other time I'd used my power, it had been when something terrifying had either attacked me or been thrown in my path. If I could manage to use my magic—and I don't mean the talking to animals portion—when I actually needed it, then that would be a bonus.

"So what do I do?" I said, sinking to my knees. I pulled the knapsack over my head and plopped it on the smooth surface beside me.

"Dip your hands in. That's all you have to do."

I quirked a brow. "So people come here to see what they fear the most?"

Mattie shook her head. It was an all-too-human move. "No, sugar. They come for all sorts of reasons. It's mainly the teenagers lookin' for a good scare that come to dip their hands in. Oh, and you."

"Thanks," I said flatly.

I pushed up my sleeves and slipped my hands below the surface. My heart thundered and a line of sweat sprinkled my brow. The hollow sound of water droplets splashing to the floor filled my ears.

Let's say I was on edge.

I had no idea what to expect, but in the back of my mind, I figured the one thing I most feared would be Rufus. I did not want to see that guy. Two times he'd tried to capture me and twice I'd escaped.

Would I manage to slip from his grasp if he tried to take me one more time?

All this filled my head as a cloud of smoke rose from the puddle. It curled and coiled, forming into a dark shape.

I watched as ebony patches of fur blazed to life. Sharp fangs, claws made to slash flesh and a deep growl echoed in the chamber.

It looked real. It smelled real. And when the werewolf sprang toward me, teeth dripping with saliva, I scrambled back and threw out my hand.

I wanted it gone, away.

The werewolf reared as if in pain. With its head arched, the creature released a heart-thundering howl and evaporated into twisting wisps of steam.

It was the same creature I'd seen in the Cobweb Forest several weeks ago. I swallowed an egg in my throat as my heart knocked like it would pound right on out of my chest.

Mattie licked her lips. "Well, the last thing I expected to see was that. I figured you'd be most afraid of a talking goat or something."

I clutched my chest. "I thought it would be Rufus."

"That makes more sense than a goat, I suppose."

I nodded. "I suppose so."

"Don't you worry, sugar. Betty watches that werewolf. That dog ain't goin' nowhere."

I rubbed goosebumps from my arms. "Good thing. Come on. My headache's gone and I think I've had enough of this place for now."

Mattie led me from the cavern.

We descended a steep slope until we reached gravel. The stretch led us to one of the main streets that wound around town. I followed Mattie until we hit a dirt road nestled between two rows of trees. The sun was slipping from sight, so I pulled out my flashlight to lend extra visibility.

"I should've brought my skillet so we could ride back," I said.

Mattie glanced up at me. "I shoulda told you to. But either way, I know a shortcut that won't take us through the cave. How's that sound?"

I shivered. "Great. Not interested in returning there anytime soon."

Just around a bend, a green cottage came into view. Gaslights lined the porch. I paused. "Is someone home?"

Mattie shook her head. "The mouse said he'd turn 'em on for us."

"Oh, okay." I stopped. "But you're sure? Axel said they might let Rufus into town for the funeral."

Mattie picked up her pace. "Then I guess we need to be hurryin'. Come on, let's go around back."

I followed her to the rear, where a set of steps led to a lower level basement door. Cobwebs framed the stairwell. Something slithered between a pair of bushes beside the house.

"Yeah, I'm not going down there," I said.

Mattie laughed. "Your mom was a chicken, too. Let me get that mouse."

Mattie meowed a few times. A second later, a small brown rodent scurried from the bushes. Oh, so that's what had been in the bushes—only a little mouse. Not a scary snake or a terrifying Rufus.

Good to know.

"This is my mistress, Pepper," Mattie said.

"Pleased to meet you," the mouse said. "My name's Dave."

Dave. The mouse. Nothing failed to surprise me anymore.

"Thank you for meeting us," I said.

Mattie crept to him. "Well? Did you bring something?"

Dave squeaked. "I was only able to find one. She used to have more, but she must've moved them."

"Moved what?" I said.

"The magic containers," Dave said, glancing up at me.

Mattie cocked her head. "According to Dave, Melbalean did work magic that took important *things* from people."

"What sort of things?" I said.

Dave disappeared into a bush. He returned, nudging something along with his nose.

"Is that an egg?" I said.

Dave squeaked out a yes.

"And this egg has something in it?" I said skeptically.

"Yes," Dave said. "It should."

I sighed. This was about the stupidest thing I'd ever heard. I was about to say thanks but no thanks, when I heard tires on dirt coming up the drive.

"Hide," Mattie said.

I scrambled behind one of the bushes. I waited, holding my breath and wincing as a branch poked me right in the ribs. The car idled in the drive. After a few moments, the vehicle backed out, heading to town.

The three of us convened again. "Take the egg," Dave prodded.

"It's not rotten, is it?" I said.

"It's magic," he insisted.

I picked up the egg and held it to the light. It was an ordinary ochre color. Nothing particularly interesting about it. Mattie nudged me. I was crouching and hadn't expected it. My grasp on the egg loosened and it slipped from my fingers.

I scrambled to catch it, but it splattered against the poured concrete sidewalk. I cowered, anticipating a huge rotting stink to waft up into the air.

Don't ask me why I thought that, but it was an egg that a mouse had given me. I didn't expect it to be the best cared for little egg on the planet.

But when the shell broke open and its contents spilled out, it wasn't a yellow yoke and some clear membrane. It was a face—a beautiful young woman with flowing black hair, dark skin, hazel eyes and high cheekbones. She was gorgeous.

I peered closer, wanting to get a better gander. "What's that?"

The mouse squeaked, "Someone's looks."

I frowned. "What do you mean?"

Mattie pawed at the shell until it completely broke away. "What he means is—Melbalean took someone's beauty in exchange for a favor."

I gasped. "So this beautiful woman gave up her looks to Melbalean? So what Peter Potion said wasn't a lie."

Mattie sat. "Don't look like it to me."

I picked at the broken fragments. "And then Melbalean hid what she stole in eggshells?"

"Least likely place someone would look," Dave said.

I nodded. "Well, that at least makes the most sense out of everything else. But why not put them in something less fragile?"

"She had them in a carton," Dave said as if that answered it all.

"Why do I even question things if they have reasonable explanations?"

Sure. If you can call stowing a person's looks in an eggshell in a carton reasonable. Am I the only person that wonders what would happen if some drunk guy broke into the house in the middle of the night looking for a midnight snack and he scrambled up one of those eggs?

For a witch who traded in faces and secrecy, that could've been a problem.

Told you I had an overactive imagination.

I gestured toward the face. "What do we do with this?"

"Put it in your water bottle," Mattie said.

I pulled a bottle from the knapsack and emptied it into the bushes. I will not lie and say I enjoyed scooping up the eggy beauty and dumping it in, but that's what happened.

I capped it and said to Dave, "Thanks so much. This is very helpful."

The mouse said his goodnights and then he dove into the hedges.

I turned to Mattie. "Okay. Let's blow this joint."

We walked down the drive and onto the main road. We'd gone about three feet when a set of headlights snapped on behind us.

My heart fluttered into my mouth. Whoever had driven up Melbalean's road hadn't left. They'd been waiting.

What if it was Rufus?

I pivoted to face the car right as a figure stepped into the darkness. "Nobody move. Hold it right there."

TWELVE

"*W*hat do you think you're doing up at Melbalean's?"

I squinted into the darkness. "Axel?"

"That's me."

I rested a palm over my pounding heart. I inhaled a deep shot of air and sank to my knees. "Oh my Lord. I thought you were Rufus or someone worse. I thought we were dead and I'm so young. There's so much I haven't experienced yet. I mean I just learned to like the animals at the pet store. There's a lot I want to do with my life."

"You're being dramatic."

"Only about the animal part."

Mattie hissed at me.

"I like animals. I love you," I said.

"That's good, sugar."

I threaded my fingers through my hair and tugged it over one shoulder. "Just what do you think you're doing? Stalking me?"

Axel scoffed. "No. I came out here to look for clues."

I kicked a pebble toward him. "I thought you said *we* needed to leave Melbalean's house alone. And would you kick off the high beams so I can see you?"

Axel flipped on the daytime running lights. He sighed as he folded his arms. "I'm pretty sure I said *you* needed to stay away."

I strode forward until I could reach out and touch the hood. "I thought it went without saying. If I was supposed to stay away, so were you."

He scrubbed a hand over his jaw. "I'm not the one who's an inexperienced witch."

"You could've invited me."

"Seems you invited yourself."

"Sure did. Wouldn't you like to know what I found?"

He eyed me and I could feel the tension building between us again. He shut his door softly and came around until he stood by one of the tires. "Was it big and scary?"

I laughed. "Big and scary I can deal with."

What a total lie.

"This," I said, "was something else." I pulled the bottle from the pack and handed it to him.

Axel's eyes widened as he realized what he was seeing. He released a low whistle. "Holy cow. So the rumors were true."

"So it appears." I paused. "But why are you here?"

He handed the bottle to me. "I was looking for you."

I quirked a brow. "Really? Why?"

Coming to tell me your deep, dark secrets? Or just to confess your undying love?

Yes, I know I needed to get a grip. We were just—whatever it was we were. Heck, I didn't even know.

"I came because I heard from the mayor," he said. "Want to get in? I'll give you a ride."

"Sure." I glanced over my shoulder. "Mattie, you coming too?"

The cat padded off toward the darkness. "Nah. I'm gonna go catch me a ground squirrel to eat. I love eating 'em. They're good grub."

"Okay." I shrugged. Axel rounded the hood. His shoulder brushed mine as he passed. He opened my door and I slid in.

When we were both strapped and ready to go, he fired up the

engine. The Mustang purred like a kitten as he threaded his way down the winding mountain toward Magnolia Cove.

"Did you get a chance to talk to the chicken company?" I said.

Axel's gaze slid toward me. "I called, but had to leave a message. They're not open on Sundays. I'll call them again tomorrow."

I worried the inside of my lip. "Do you think they'll be able to help?"

He shifted gears as we hit a steep curve. "Hopefully."

"Betty had Garrick take her chicken. She told them that it held the key to who killed Melbalean."

"Good lie," Axel said.

"It did get her released. She's nothing if not savvy."

He didn't say anything. The cabin smelled like him—musky with a hint of pine. His hair was pulled back though a couple of super sexy strands fell over his right eye. The dimple in his cheek popped in as he hit the clutch.

"You heard from the mayor?"

Axel inhaled. He adjusted his seat belt as if what I said made him uncomfortable. "Yes. Melbalean's funeral is tomorrow. The council decided to let Rufus attend."

I gulped. I wiped slick palms on my thighs. I didn't know why I was surprised. Axel had told me it was possible. Hearing that Rufus would be in town was nothing new.

"Will he be able to roam free? Do whatever he wants?" I said.

Axel slanted his head toward me. "No. From what I understand he'll have some supervision, though I'm not sure what. I've already told Garrick about your situation with Rufus and he's on alert. And I'll be around tomorrow during the day."

"What about tomorrow night?"

Axel glanced at the road. "I've got some work to do."

"But Rufus should be gone by then, right? They're only letting him in for the funeral, aren't they?"

Axel shook his head. "He's got twenty-four hours in town."

My head dropped to the seat rest. "Seriously? Twenty-four hours? He could get into all kinds of trouble during that time."

Axel nodded. "Like I said, I'll be around. And you'll have your family to protect you."

"That's true. Betty will have her shotgun. There's no way Rufus would be stupid enough to try anything with her nearby."

"So...you want to grab some dinner?"

He said it right as my stomach rumbled. I flashed him a bright smile. "You got that right."

~

THE LOOKS we garnered when we entered Spellin' Skillet were completely different than anything I'd experienced with Axel before. While half the women drooled over Mr. Sexy, as they liked to refer to him, the men sneered.

Axel kept his head tipped down as the waitress led us to a room in the back, where they apparently kept a table open for him at all times.

I ordered a salad with mandarin oranges, goat cheese and sugared pecans, while Axel ordered a steak.

"So what do you think about the witch's looks we found?" I said.

Axel glanced up, his eyes full of interest. "Wonder who's it is."

"No clue." I drummed my fingers on the table. "Do you think that's why Melbalean was killed?"

He shrugged. "No idea. For all I know, someone put a spell on the hen to kill her and then blame Betty."

I scoffed. "Do you really think that's possible?"

"It's about as crazy as sticking someone's face in an egg."

"That's true. The mouse, the one who found the egg, said there used to be more. Could still be. Might just have to look in the right places."

Axel glared at me. "Stay away. Rufus is about to be in town. He'll be going there. You're asking for trouble."

"I know, I'm trying to figure this out. I don't want the police to come back and point a finger at Betty. Maybe there's something they missed at the booth. Maybe there's a clue that was left there."

He sliced into his steak. "Like what? A feather?"

I smirked. "Very funny." I took a long sip of sweet tea. "I don't know. Something. Maybe we could stop by on our way to my house?"

"No."

"Please?" I said cheerfully.

"No."

"Pretty please, with sugar on top?"

He shook his head.

And then I reached under and squeezed his knee. Axel jerked back, nearly leaping from the table.

"That wasn't the reaction I was going for," I said.

Not that I was trying to seduce him, only convince him that I was on his side.

Axel cleared his throat, took another bite of his steak and shot me dark, searching look as he said, "Okay."

I nearly jumped for joy.

"But it doesn't mean anything," he said.

"Of course not."

I couldn't help but hum to myself as we cruised toward downtown. "I'm sorry I touched you," I said.

His mouth quirked. "Don't be sorry. I'm an idiot for reacting the way I did."

We slid into a spot with a clear view of the festival. The lights were off. "I guess the festival cleared out early tonight."

Axel nodded. "I think Melbalean's death put a damper on most of the festivities. Soon as things settle, it'll pick back up. You'll see."

"Great." I slid my fingers over the handle and started to shove open the door.

"Wait."

"Yes?" I said, turning back.

Axel's face was only a breath from mine. He brushed a strand of hair from my cheek. "Pepper," he said, his voice low, "there are so many things I want to tell you."

I nodded. "I'm pretty easy to talk to."

He chuckled. "That's not what I mean. For so long, I've pushed people away."

"You were friends with my uncle."

He glanced down. Rows of thick eyelashes brushed his cheeks. "That's not what I meant. I mean with women."

I giggled uncomfortably. Deciding I sounded horrible, like a wheezing ox, I cleared my throat. "I knew that. I knew what you meant. Obviously with women. Not men."

"You're the first women I've met in some time that I want to get close to. That I want to spend time with."

"You never call," I said.

He gritted his teeth. "I want to get to know you. I want you to know me, but I don't want you to be scared."

I narrowed my eyes until I felt my brows pinch. "Scared? What about you could scare me?"

Something fluttered in the corner of my eye. I glanced up and saw a shadow slice through the night.

"Who's that?" I said, leaning sideways to get a better view.

"A person," Axel said.

I quirked my brow in annoyance. "I know it's a person. I'm wondering who it is."

He flashed me a devilish smile. "Let's take a look." I eased open the door and followed Axel onto the sidewalk. "Where'd it go?" I whispered.

Axel narrowed his eyes as if he wanted me to be quiet. I shrugged, as if to silently tell him I was sorry.

A second later, the shadow blurred in front of me. "Ah!" I jumped.

"Sorry, I didn't mean to scare y'all," came the voice.

Out of the darkness stepped a man. I squinted at the figure. "Lane?"

Light from a streetlamp splashed onto his shoulders. "That's me."

"What are you doing out here?"

He rubbed his neck and that's when I noticed he was wearing a hat and the hat didn't cover the bald patch at the base of his head.

Oh, dear Lord, Betty had balded him.

I know that's not a word but it sure seemed to fit.

"I'm looking for a small violet. I needed it for some, um, cosmetic things. I thought I saw one out here earlier, but now I don't anymore. Anyways," he rubbed the spot again, "y'all don't have to tell Amelia that you saw me out here. I mean, I'm going to see her tomorrow, I'm sure, as long as I can get things straightened out. We were both feeling poorly tonight and didn't end up going out."

Poor guy. He didn't want my cousin to know he was bald. I nearly laughed. She didn't want him to know she was bald, either.

Boy, these two were perfect for each other.

I glanced over at Axel. "Want to help him find some violets?"

He shot me a smile. "Why not?"

So we spent the next ten minutes helping Lane. It was a small purple and yellow flower that he wanted. Most of them had wilted during the summer, but he swore there was a small patch that he'd seen.

"That was crazy about Melbalean," Lane said.

I stopped. "You knew her?" I shot Axel a look.

Lane scoured the grass, looking. "Oh, yeah. She and my grand-mother were friends, but they had a falling out. From what I under-stand, on my Grandma's deathbed she blamed Melbalean for her predicament."

"You mean her death," Axel said.

"That's right."

"Did you know your grandmother well?" I said.

"I never knew her. She passed long before I was born."

I felt like I needed to question him delicately. "Do *you* think Melbalean caused her death?"

Lane looked uncertain. "No telling. According to Grandma, Melbalean cursed our family."

"How so?" I said.

Lane said, "She gave us webbed feet."

I paused. "Really?"

Lane laughed. "Yeah."

"Are they still webbed?" Axel said. "Now that's Melbalean's dead?"

Lane nodded. "Oh yeah."

We finished up, eventually finding the violets in a small patch of dirt near where Melbalean had been killed.

"Now, why didn't I think to look for them here?" Lane said.

"Beats me," I said.

Finding what he needed, I hopped in the car with Axel, who stared at Lane as he walked down the sidewalk, heading toward the inn, where he was staying.

"Something about that guy," Axel said, cranking the engine.

"What?"

He shook his head. "I don't trust him."

"Why? He was just looking for the flowers."

"No, he wasn't," he said.

"What do you mean?"

Axel nodded toward Lane's pocket. "He already had a bunch of the flowers. They were hanging out of his pocket."

"So you're saying he lied."

Axel's gaze sharpened. "Yep. And I plan on finding out why."

THIRTEEN

$\mathcal{W}$e reached the house a minute later. I glanced at my watch and smiled. "Ha. Not quite ten o'clock. We're early."

Axel glanced at his watch and cringed. "I'm on military time and according to it we're thirty seconds late."

"Ah!"

I bolted from the Mustang with Axel behind me. I leaped up the porch stairs and crashed through the front door.

Betty sat in her rocker, the shotgun slung over her knees. The corncob pipe was smoking up a fog in the house. "You're late."

"I thought you weren't feeling well," I said, dumping my purse on the couch.

"I'm always up when it comes to making sure you youngsters are in the house."

What? Am I five? I haven't been called a youngster since, well, I don't know—the beginning of time?

Axel strode in. "Sorry, we're late. We ran into Lane."

Betty's eyes sparked. "Oh? Did he have any hair?"

"No," I said, "and I think he's searching for flowers to grow it back."

Betty scratched her chin. "That could work. Anyway, glad you're safe. Now get upstairs, you're heading out early tomorrow."

I rolled my eyes. I said goodnight to Axel, feeling tension flare between us. I wanted to reach out and touch his arm, or at least peck his cheek, but with Betty glaring at us, neither of those two things happened. Anyway, I slinked upstairs as Betty the matron said, and set my alarm so I could find Mayor Potion in the morning.

By the time my head hit the pillow, I was nearly out. My thoughts drifted to the conversation with Axel, and how he didn't want me to be afraid of him.

What was there to be afraid of?

It was my last thought as sleep finally overtook me.

IT WAS SURPRISINGLY easy to wake up early the next morning. Mattie the cat had somehow sneaked back into the house and was laying on the window seat curled into a ball. I tugged on some clothes and headed out to find the mayor.

He was laying in the arms of Amaryllis Snitch, the witch statue. I covered the mayor with the blanket. He moaned and grumbled to life. At the foot of the statue, I noticed a small cameo pin. I picked it up and squinted until my eyes adjusted to the image. When the picture sharpened, I sucked in air and nearly dropped the pin to the ground.

It was the same face as the one Melbalean's egg contained. At least, it looked like it. The egg face was a bit distorted, but they nearly matched.

Mmm. I wondered what that was all about. I tucked the cameo in my pocket and helped the mayor to life. I guided him to his house, where he made me a cup of coffee.

"The more I find out about Melbalean, the more I think she duped this entire town," I said.

"What makes you say that?" he said.

I drummed my fingers on the lacquered bar-style counter that separated his kitchen from the living room. I was finger-pinching close to tell him about the beauty we'd found in the eggshell, but I decided to skip it.

"There's a man I met—Lane Longmire, who says Melbalean cursed his family to all have webbed feet."

Mayor Potion hooted with laughter. "Webbed feet?"

I twisted the ends of my hair in embarrassment. "Did I say something wrong? Do they not have webbed feet?"

He shook his head, cleared his throat and spat in the sink. "Now they may have webbed feet but if Melbalean cursed the Longmires it doesn't have nothin' to do with a little skin between the toes."

I quirked a brow. "What do you mean?"

"Those Longmires may have 'long' in their name, but there's nothing long about their lives."

I cracked the knuckles on my right hand. "Sorry?"

Potion shook his head. "They don't live past the age of thirty. If Melbalean cursed them it was to live a short life."

I leaned forward and stared straight into Peter's bloodshot eyes. "Are you joking?"

"No ma'am, I am not joking. I may be a drunk and a mayor, but I do not joke. Not about this sort of thing. Ask anyone. They'll tell you. Longmires from around here, or who have relatives from here, don't live past thirty. I don't know who this fellow is you're talking about, but I'd take a risk and say he's one of them."

It was definitely worth asking Betty about. She had found Lane on the dating site, but where was he actually from? And was he affected by the curse? If he was, Axel and I had found him snooping near where Melbalean's body was discovered. Was he returning to the crime scene for some reason? Or was it simply coincidence?

So many questions.

I left Mayor Potion's house and walked home. I didn't bump into Axel on a morning run, which almost made me a little sad. It was fine. I had lots of work to do. Besides, he said he'd be around because today was Melbalean's funeral and that meant one thing—Rufus would be in town.

My stomach pretzeled at the thought of that rock-star-looking guy slinking around town.

I got home, patted Jennie the guard-vine and entered the house. Betty was sitting beside the fire, looking tired.

"Are you okay?" I said.

She smacked her lips. "Fine. Just a little tired today. I think those coppers put something in my water. Juiced me somehow."

I quirked a brow at how ridiculous I thought that was, but whatever. "You sure you don't need to see a doctor?"

She shook her head. "I know every potion there is, I don't need to see a witch doctor."

"I meant a real one. You know, not a witch."

Betty dismissed me with a wave of her hand. "Bah. No."

I sank into a chair opposite her. "Did you know that the Longmires don't live past thirty?"

Betty laid her beady eyes on me. "Don't tell your cousin."

I stifled a laugh. Clearly, she knew. "So Lane is related to other Longmires from around here?"

"A cousin." Betty's eyes sparked. "So he was pretty bald, huh?"

I nodded. "The bald spell worked, if that's what you're asking."

"Good. Now they can be twins."

I shook my head. "My guess is they'll be avoiding each other like the plague in heat."

Betty stared at me. "Are you suggesting the plague is sexually active?"

I cringed. "It wasn't a very good comparison, was it?"

She pulled the blanket tighter around her shoulders. "Next time, I'd stick to white on rice or white on grits—makes more sense."

I went upstairs to get ready for the day. By the time I'd showered, eaten breakfast and checked on Amelia, who was not coming out of her room, by the way, it was about time to head to work.

I shot Betty a look before leaving. "If you're not any better when I get home, we're going to find you a doctor—a normal one."

Betty frowned at me, but said nothing.

I left the house and made it to Familiar Place in about five minutes.

I saw my cousin Carmen, who owned the sweet shop and gave her a wave.

"I've created new jelly bean flavors," she called to me.

My stomach rumbled from the thought. "I'll check them out later."

Carmen smiled. "You're going to love these—Lingering Lemon, Powerful Peach and Lasting Licorice."

"Oh, okay. I might skip the Lasting Licorice."

She laughed. "Stop on by."

I gave one last wave and headed inside the store. The animals slowly came to life. The kittens stretched and the puppies in the window yawned. The birds fluttered their wings and the lizards blinked.

Yep. I even sold familiar lizards. I had yet to see a witch buy one, but it was bound to happen. Why else would Uncle Donovan have stocked them?

I fed them and cleaned and refreshed all the water bowls. I glanced at the floor and noticed that the feedbag the chicken had come with sat in a corner. It looked like regular old seed, so I threw some into the bird dishes for the African grey and the other exotic birds I carried.

I cleaned the counters and the windows and feeling a wave of satisfaction at the lemon scented, gleaming store, I brushed my hands and smiled, awaiting my first customer.

Something black flashed outside the windows. I stopped and stared, trying to get a better look.

I wasn't able to see what it was until the door opened and the bell above tinkled the arrival of a new customer.

He stood in the doorway, clad in black leather from head to foot. My heart thundered in my mouth as my gaze dragged from his thick ebony boots to his black jacket, fingers drenched in silver rings, long dark hair that was teased up and eyes rimmed in black liner.

Rufus.

He took a step forward. "I've been looking for you, Pepper Dunn."

FOURTEEN

I knew this had been coming. Felt it in my marrow. Felt it all the way to the tiny cells in the pits of my lungs. I knew Rufus would be walking into my life.

And as much as it scared me, the rockstar wannabe made me angry.

Like he wanted me to be afraid. Wanted me to fear him.

And y'all know what? That crap ain't cool.

I crossed my arms and tamped down the fear threatening to scramble up my throat. "You've been looking for me? That's funny, 'cause I haven't been looking for you."

A slow smiled curved on his lips. "Last time we met, I said I needed you to come with me. That hasn't changed." His voice was thick, rich like butter. Like he used it to seduce people and then play vampire on them.

Which was stupid because he wasn't a vampire.

Dude had some issues.

"I'm not going anywhere with you," I said smartly.

He moved like a blur and in less than a second, he stood in front of me. All I could see were those dark eyes of his.

I didn't have time to be afraid or time to react. His hand shot out and wrapped around my arm.

Now I had time to feel the fear.

It sizzled up my spine as his dark eyes held mine. I gulped but the air stuck. It wouldn't enter my lungs and it wouldn't leave.

"You will be mine," he said.

My brain hiccupped. It wouldn't move forward or backward. It was like I was frozen in time and place, suspended on an invisible string. Rufus was the puppeteer and I was the marionette, dancing for his amusement.

Boy, that really burned my biscuits.

I tried to move, but couldn't. All I could do was stare into the dark eyes and watch as Rufus smiled. A shiver pierced my heart.

He tugged me forward. I couldn't stop him.

Suddenly the birds perched behind me squawked and cawed. The air kicked up as half a dozen wings surrounded us.

Rufus lurched as the African grey clipped at his eyes. Rufus drew away, but the bird raked its talons over his face. He screamed. The rest of the birds descended, snapping at his arms, his shoulders. One little parakeet even fluttered around his legs.

Rufus batted and clawed the air, trying to get them off him.

"Witch," he screamed. "Get your attack birds off me!"

But I hadn't done anything. I stepped away, letting them have at him. Y'all, you and I know that Rufus's intentions weren't anything golden and warm—they were dark and evil.

Feathers filled the air. Rufus continued yelling as he darted toward the exit. His fingers scraped the door handle until he grabbed hold and threw it open.

The birds blew back as if hit by a wind. Rufus darted from the building and the creatures shrank away. Rufus disappeared down the street. The parakeets, macaws and African greys squawked and chattered, turning around to look at me.

I could feel their energy. It was like something had taken hold of them and they wanted blood. If they couldn't have Rufus's, then they wanted someone else's.

I backed up and flared out my arms. "Hold it right there. Y'all better think twice about even coming one step toward me with those sharp little talons of yours. Y'all even think about harming me and I'll starve you. And I'm not trying to be cruel to animals, but it's called self-preservation. I think Darwin wrote about it."

Heck, I had no idea who wrote about it, and I'm pretty darned sure it wasn't Darwin, but it sounded official.

They continued flapping, but the earlier frenzy vanished. They drifted back slowly, going to perch on their rests.

"What happened to y'all?" I said once they'd settled.

The African grey's feathers rose on its neck. "He was a vile, evil man. We had to stop him."

"But y'all've never acted that way before."

"You've never been attacked before," one of the puppies said.

"I'll claw his eyes out," a kitten said. "Get him back here."

"Okay, hold on there, Rover," I said.

The kitten clawed the wire cage. "I'm a cat, thank you very much. Not a dog. Do not call me by one of their names."

"Sorry."

I sank onto a stool. My hands trembled. I flexed my fingers, trying to stop the shaking. I was a bundle of nerves. Raw energy ripped through me. That had been close.

Too close.

And what the heck? Wasn't someone supposed to be watching Rufus?

The door banged open. Axel strode in, eyes blazing, shoulder muscles tight as if he'd been working out.

His gaze dragged from the mess of feathers to me, and I apparently looked crumpled and worn, because in one, two, three long strides Axel was beside me, pulling me from the stool, wrapping his arms around me and pressing his lips to mine.

Wait. What the heck?

I wiggled from his grasp. "Just what the heck do you think you're doing?"

His blue eyes flashed confusion. "What do you mean? I'm kissing you. I was worried sick."

I fisted a hand on my hip. "Now you're kissing me? We spend a whole night holding hands at a fair and you tell me you're complicated, but you're kissing me now?"

He rubbed his neck. Dots of red bloomed on his cheeks. "One of the detectives radioed in that Rufus had been seen here."

Then it hit me. He was worried.

Worried.

About me.

I threw my arms around his neck and pressed my lips to his. Who the heck cared about all the rest? Axel was worried about me.

I guess I already knew that. I mean, it wasn't exactly news to me, or anything. He'd said he'd look in on me. But the fact was, he was worried enough that it broke a barrier between us. Worried enough that he kissed me.

And boy, was it hot.

Yep. Hot right in the middle of a pet shop.

Weird, right?

We broke after a few seconds. I gulped some air and pressed away from his chest. "Wow. I didn't know you felt that way."

He raked his fingers through his thick, wavy locks. "I guess when I heard about Rufus, it got the better of me."

I nodded. "I guess so." I tossed him a bright smile full of teeth. "I can handle it."

Axel ran a finger along my jaw. "Good. Cause there's a lot to handle."

I frowned. "When did this conversation suddenly go from G to R-rated?"

He chuckled. "You're misunderstanding what I'm saying," he said in his light, Southern drawl. "That's not where my mind went."

I shook my head. "Oh, me neither. My mind did not go anywhere bad. Not at all. We're totally in this PG-13 movie together."

"Okay," he said.

Feeling like a geek for going over the deep end of the conversation,

I decided to reel it in. "So that was Rufus. The birds stopped him. I don't know what got into them, but they suddenly attacked. They saved me."

Axel's jaw tightened. "It's worse than I thought. I didn't think he'd try anything during the daylight, but obviously, I was wrong. Listen, I think you should close up shop early if you can." He glanced at his watch. "The funeral's about to start any minute, and that along with the graveside service will probably last two hours. But after that, Rufus'll be on the loose again."

I scoffed. "I can't close at noon. The festival is still going on. There are folks in town who want a familiar. That's business I'd be giving up. I can't do it."

Axel sighed. "Okay. I've some things to do and I'll return and spend the afternoon, but then I want you under Betty's protection for the rest of the night. No way would Rufus try something on her turf."

I nodded dumbly as he brushed his lips across my forehead. Heat blazed across my skin where his mouth touched me. He left and I found myself surrounded by a floor full of feathers.

I turned to the birds. "Well, looks like I've got some cleaning up to do."

AXEL DID return as he said. As the sun slinked toward late afternoon, he started pacing.

"It's going to be okay," I said. "I'll be fine. Rufus won't get me."

He crossed his arms and gave me a smile that made a shiver rip down my spine—in a good way. "I know. I just want to get you home."

I glanced at the wall clock and said, "It's ten minutes to closing. I think we can go."

I locked up the animals after bidding them goodbye and we started toward Betty's. We reached the house a few minutes later.

"Do you want to come in? I'm sure she's prepared an amazing dinner. Sometimes on Mondays she makes chicken and dumplings. It's pretty awesome."

He brushed a strand of hair from my cheek. "Wish I could, but I've got things to do. Be safe."

He gave me a quick peck on the lips and disappeared down the street. I barely had a chance to wave goodbye before he was out of sight.

I marched inside and found Betty moving around slowly but surely. She did have dinner ready and it was chicken and dumplings. Axel didn't know what he was missing out on.

"You've been kissing," Betty grumbled. "If I felt better, I'd take a switch to your bottom, but seeing as you're an adult and I don't feel that great, I'll leave it."

I dropped my purse. "I thought I said if you didn't feel better I was taking you to a doctor."

She waved the air dismissively. "Doctor, schmoctor. If I don't feel better in the morning we'll see one, but my guess is I should be fine by then."

Cordelia and Amelia appeared. Amelia's hair was still short.

"I've tried everything," she said, pouring a glass of tea. "I can't seem to get anything to stick. How am I supposed to see Lane like this?"

Cordelia's mouth curved into a sly smile. "You could always admit what happened."

Amelia's jaw dropped. "Admit I had hair extensions? No way. Lane is the first guy I've liked in forever. I'm not going to risk my happiness over a bit of hair."

Betty and I exchanged a glance. Someone kicked me under the table. I'm guessing it was Betty. "What?" I whispered.

"Tell her," Betty said.

I rolled my eyes. "Do I have to?"

"Tell me what?" Amelia said, eyes wide with panic.

I pushed the food around on my plate. "Lane's lost his hair."

"No," Amelia screamed.

"I'm afraid it's true. I saw him last night."

Amelia pointed at Betty. "You better fix him."

Betty shrugged. "I did fix him. Now you match."

She cackled like the Wicked Witch of the West.

I clicked my tongue. "She does have a point. Lane might not care that you don't have as much hair as he thought."

Amelia pushed back from the table. "No way. I've got to keep up my looks. At least until he leaves. I can't lose all my hair."

Cordelia shook her glass until the ice clinked together. "Tell him you'll grow it back."

Amelia sank her face into her hands. "It's horrible. There's no way I can see him again."

Betty folded her napkin on the table. "By tomorrow morning, when hopefully I'm feeling better, we'll try again, see if I can get it to grow. I'll fix Lane's hair too. Don't worry. You won't have to date a baldy."

"Thank you," Amelia said. "I've got enough to worry about without having to add my appearance to it."

We all stared at her. "What else do you have to worry about?" I said.

"Oh, you know—am I mysterious enough to Lane? Do I laugh like an idiot? Is a booger hanging out of my nose?"

"Just don't eat it," Cordelia quipped.

"Very funny," Amelia said.

Betty braced her hands on the table. "Girls, I was hoping it wouldn't come to this, I really was, but it doesn't look like I have a choice."

Amelia dabbed her mouth with her napkin. "About what?"

"About tonight," Betty said.

I jabbed a dumpling with my fork. "What about tonight?"

"It's the full moon," Cordelia said.

For some reason, nothing was sinking in. "What about it?"

Betty's eyes hardened. "Girls, I was hoping I'd feel better. I was hoping I'd be able to do it on my own, because as y'all know, this town would fall on its rear end without me, but I don't see another way around it."

"Isn't there someone else?" Amelia said.

"Like who?" Cordelia shot back. "No one else knows she does it."

"We know," Amelia said.

Cordelia smirked. "And we don't say a word because she told us she'd hang us upside down naked in front of town hall if we told anyone."

I flattened my palms on the table. "What are y'all talking about?"

Betty folded her hands. "Tonight, Pepper, you have the most important job in all of Magnolia Cove."

I shrugged. "I thought I already did by owning the familiar shop."

"It's not as important as this," Betty said.

"Yeah," Cordelia said, "the only reason we know is because she told us, but no one else does because that could put her life in danger."

I glanced at Betty. "Put your life in danger? How?"

Betty leaned forward. "Tonight, you have the most important job in all of Magnolia Cove."

"As you've said. So what is it?"

Betty's eyes sharpened as she said, "Tonight you guard the werewolf. Make sure he doesn't get loose because if you do, you'll put the entire town in jeopardy."

FIFTEEN

$\mathcal{I}$ rose. "What? We're supposed to guard the werewolf? No way. No how. That thing almost bit my head off last time I saw it. There is no way on all of God's green earth and then some that I'm going to guard a werewolf."

"It's not like you won't have silver bullets," Betty mumbled. "What do you think? I'm going to put you in a dangerous situation?"

I nodded. "Yes. Yes, I do think you're going to do that. Worse, I don't think you care."

"Oh, she cares," Cordelia said. "Enough to give us silver bullets."

Betty pointed at her. "Watch it, or you'll be out your dinner."

Cordelia gave her plate a bored look. "I have to watch my figure anyway."

Betty's hard glare ripped into me, making me feel bad for not immediately jumping on the let's-go-watch-a-werewolf bandwagon.

"Okay," I said, hanging my head. "I'll help watch the werewolf."

"Good," Betty said. "'Cause you girls are going to be late."

She crossed to the hearth and picked up the shotgun resting on its butt beside near it. She cracked it open and pulled out the slugs. She looped her finger in the air and two more slugs hovered in the air. Betty thumbed them into the barrels and shut it tight.

"He'll show up right before you and chain himself. Don't look at him. Don't watch the transformation."

I raked my fingers nervously through my hair. "Why? Is it bad luck or something? Will I turn into a werewolf if I see someone else change into one?"

"No," Betty snapped, "it's just plain rude. Would you want someone to watch you?"

"I guess not."

"The only rule is, make sure he doesn't escape. No matter what, the wolf is not allowed to be unchained. He can't control what he does in the animal state. So what's the rule?" Her steely gaze landed on me.

I wagged my finger at her as if I were a four-year-old giving her what for. "No setting the wolf free. You don't have to worry about me on that one. I won't be letting that creature loose. I'm scared to death of it."

Betty dragged her gaze from me to Cordelia and Amelia. "Girls, get your skillets. You've got some flying to do."

I HOPPED on my cast iron skillet and readied to follow Amelia and Cordelia to the Cobweb forest. The moon hadn't started to rise yet, but it would be soon.

"Come on," Cordelia said, "we need to put the pedal to the metal."

Wind whisked my hair as we rode through the quiet night. We reached the forest and landed inside a square copse of hedges.

A slab of concrete had been poured in the middle and a chain secured to it.

Cordelia pointed to a corner. "Let's stand there until he comes and changes."

There was one burning question I couldn't keep inside me any longer. "Who is it? Who's the wolf?"

Right then, a figure appeared from the other side of the hedges. He had arrived. The werewolf.

I couldn't see his face and that's what I wanted. I gave him a hard glance as Amelia tugged my sleeve.

"We're not supposed to look."

I frowned. "Right."

Poop. Rain on my parade, why don't you?

I glanced at my feet as I heard the shuffling of clothes and the chain being secured. I didn't want to stare at a naked man, so I waited, watching my toes.

Then the ripping began. It sounded like bones breaking and crushing. Skin ripped. The gasps that the man released scared me more than the sound of muscle tearing and sewing itself into new shapes and sizes.

I held my ears, not wanting to hear too much because, to be honest y'all, I thought I might throw up.

After a minute or two, Amelia poked me in the ribs. I glanced up to see a snarling, pawing werewolf.

"Holy shrimp and grits," I said.

"I thought you'd see it before," Cordelia said.

"I had, but not quite like this."

Moonlight sliced into the copse, lighting the animal. Powerful jaws clenched as the creature growled. Massive legs extended from a thick body. The wolf's muscles quivered and twitched, making me feel as if the animal wanted to spring for us, but knew the chain kept it locked in place.

The creature growled, glaring right at us.

"What are we supposed to do?" Amelia said, "We can't stand in this corner all night."

"We can move," Cordelia said. "It's not like he can break free."

Amelia toed forward and the wolf lunged for her.

Look, I was not about to spend an entire night afraid of some stupid werewolf. I grabbed the shotgun from Cordelia, took a step and said, "Listen here, you leave us alone and we'll leave you alone."

The wolf's gaze switched from the shotgun to me. It cocked its head as I talked.

"We're here to make sure nothing happens, so quiet down. I'm not feeling like using these silver bullets, but if I have to, I will."

The beast dropped to the concrete. It wrapped one paw over the other and panted.

"Do you think it needs water?" Amelia said.

Cordelia glared at her. "Sure. Go get it some."

"I was just wondering," Amelia whimpered. "It's a perfectly legitimate question."

"Not when there's a werewolf involved," I said.

Cordelia patted my shoulder. "Good work. Wow. You're some animal tamer."

I handed her the shotgun. "It probably has something to do with my ability to talk to animals more than anything else."

Amelia eyed the creature. "I don't know. He seems to like you."

I sat on the soft grass and stretched my legs in front of me. "Do y'all know who it is?"

They exchanged a look. Cordelia spoke. "We do, but we're not allowed to say."

I frowned. "Why not?"

"It's weird," Amelia said, "It's not like it's a secret in town. Everyone knows who he is, but we don't talk about it."

"Why not?"

Cordelia plopped beside me and set the shotgun down, pointing it in the wolf's direction. "We're not supposed to."

"You've already said that," I pointed out.

"Okay," Amelia said, "I'll tell her." She leaned against the hedges, which were so thick they were nearly wall-like. "When he came to town, he was being chased by a band of witches. Some of our own. Well, not exactly our own, but witches. They said he was killing livestock. Because he's also a witch, Magnolia Cove took him in, but our police did their own investigation."

I rested my head on the hedge. "What'd they find?"

"That he wasn't guilty," Cordelia said. "So we let him stay. He lives here, and even though he's never done anything wrong, there are folks who don't trust him. They think he's a killer or that he's capable of it."

I glanced at the massive jaws. "He's definitely capable of it...So who is it?"

"So," Amelia answered, huffing out a breath, "the town decided the people who already knew about his condition could remain in the know. But to stop any unjust prejudice against him, the council deemed it illegal to tell anyone else that he can transform."

"That is so stupid," I said.

Amelia and Cordelia both laughed. The wolf's ears pricked toward us.

I tossed my head from side to side. "You would think it would keep the town safer if everyone knew who he was."

"It stops bias," Amelia said. "At least that's what they say. If someone knew what he was, they could blame almost any crime on him. That's why Betty watches over him every full moon and that's also why it's all kept very hush, hush."

I shrugged. "Whatever floats your boat, I guess. It seems to me that the more people know, the safer the whole town would be."

"It's for his own protection," Cordelia said.

"I get it. I just think it's weird." I paused. "So how're we doing this? Are we taking sleep shifts?"

Amelia's eyes sparkled in the moonlight. "Great idea, that way I don't look like a total hag tomorrow when I get my new hair in."

I laughed. "Yeah, that sounds about right."

Cordelia rubbed her forehead. "Amelia takes first shift. I'll take second—which is the worst one—"

"—Thank you for bearing such a burden," Amelia joked.

Cordelia rolled her eyes. "You're welcome. Pepper, you get third shift."

"Sounds good. Wake me when it's my turn."

I rolled over onto my side, unsure exactly how well I would sleep on the ground. But before I knew it, Cordelia was shaking me awake.

"It's your turn," she said.

I stretched and yawned, working a stiff kink from my neck. Oh, my Lord. I felt like I'd fallen asleep in a child-sized box. Every muscle hurt to move.

Cordelia handed me the shotgun. "It's been pretty quiet. It should be an easy few hours for you."

I rose and rolled my shoulders, shook out my legs. "What should I do when he starts to change?"

"Same thing. Don't watch. He'll unlock himself. He has the key."

I agreed. "Okay."

I paced from side to side as she curled into a ball to sleep. Amelia already snoozed soundly, letting out little snores now and then.

The wolf watched me at first, but then turned his face away as if my padding to and fro was too boring for him.

Time passed slowly. After I tired of pacing, I sat for a while, watching the beast.

"Do you know me?" I said to it.

The wolf cocked an ear toward me. I knew it was stupid, talking to it. I had no idea if I knew the creature.

But I wondered...was the man who lived in town in there somewhere? Or was this just a beast?

I rose and crept forward until I reached the edge of the slab, which I knew to be the creature's barrier.

"Are you in there?"

The wolf rose. I immediately backed away. Right. I might know how far the beast could walk, but that didn't mean I was one hundred percent certain it still couldn't kill me.

The creature crossed to me. It sniffed the air as if drinking in my scent. It glanced at me for a long time, holding my gaze.

"Who are you?" I said.

The wolf lowered to its haunches and rested its head on the slab. I wondered...Could I pet it?

Okay. Right. Like, clearly I was out of my gourd—but I felt a string unwinding between us, connecting us together.

I extended my hand.

The beast growled.

Well, I guess that answered that.

I tucked my hand in my pocket as the creature rose, growling as it padded in the opposite direction. The fur on its back rose stiffly.

I peered into the darkness, but I saw nothing. Yet the werewolf continued to growl, low and guttural.

With the shotgun clenched between my hands, I crossed around to see what the heck could make a werewolf's fur stand on end. I'm guessing a friendly neighborhood squirrel wouldn't exactly do that.

The beast snarled. I wasn't sure what to do. Wait? Go look?

Probably I shouldn't look. I mean, I was here to guard the werewolf until dawn. That was my job.

Turned out, I didn't have to wait.

A figure burst through the hedges, coming to rest inside the open square. A blue ball of light flickered from his fingers. The serpentine smile sent a shiver ripping along my spine.

"Rufus," I said.

His gaze narrowed. "I said I'd get you."

SIXTEEN

I bolted toward my cousins. I had to wake them, get them to safety.

A blue light shot out in front of me and encircled the two women like a band.

I whirled around. Rufus slinked forward. "Don't worry. They're not harmed, though they'll sleep through this."

I gritted my teeth. "What do you want from me?"

He slanted his head. "Why, your mind, of course. You're a head witch. Knew the moment I saw you. What power. You don't even know how to use it. Such a waste."

I leveled the shotgun at him. Sweat sprinkled my brow and my knees rattled. "Leave me be. Go now."

The werewolf snapped at Rufus. Rufus glanced at the beast. "What? Angry you can't help her? Now, now. It'll all be okay."

His gaze swiveled to the weapon and me. "You can't use that against me."

"Oh, I can't?"

Rufus glided over and tapped the barrel. A blue spark lit the end and I could feel his power like a low hum vibrating the metal. I had the distinct impression if I attempted to pull the trigger while pointing at Rufus, the gun wouldn't discharge.

And when it came right down to it, I didn't know if I had the guts to shoot anybody, anyway. That seemed horrible and bloody and terrible.

I narrowed my eyes. "I might not be able to shoot you, but there's something else I can shoot."

"What's that?" he asked, his voice carrying a lilt of fake innocence.

I aimed the shotgun at the chain holding the werewolf. "This."

The barrel exploded as gunpowder and silver spewed from the opening. The gun kicked my shoulder like a donkey that had just fueled up on breakfast.

When I was little, my dad would take me to his parent's farm for Christmas. We'd always go a few days ahead of the holiday, right when school let out. There, my grandad and I would shoot mistletoe out of trees. You see mistletoe is a parasite and it grows on branches— way up in the branches.

I'd shoot and after a few hours, we'd load up a barrelful and take it to the farmer's market and sell it to folks. Who the heck didn't want real mistletoe to kiss under for Christmas?

As you can imagine, it was totally popular.

And that also meant I knew how to point, aim and shoot a shotgun without missing. Which also meant that when the slug connected with the chain, the metal exploded.

And the werewolf was free.

The beast leaped toward Rufus, who was clearly having a very bad day when it came to animals. Rufus barely had time to throw a handful of blue light to the ground. He disappeared in a flash of smoke.

Then I realized something very, very, bad.

The werewolf was loose.

The one thing I wasn't supposed to let happen, I let happen.

The wolf threw back its head and howled. I heard Cordelia and Amelia stir and in the distance, the horizon lightened.

Daylight cracked the sky.

The wolf glanced at me. One paw moved in my direction. I leveled the shotgun at it. Without a flicker of doubt in its eyes, the beast lunged into the forest.

"Up," I yelled. "It's loose! The wolf is loose!"

I didn't wait to see if my cousins heard. I grabbed my skillet and threw one leg over it. In half a second I was zooming over the trees, the shotgun slung across my back. It took maybe fifteen seconds to find the wolf. He ran at full speed and was heading toward town.

I glanced at the horizon. The moon was slinking, but not fast enough.

"Please. Please don't do anything stupid," I said to the wolf.

This was all my fault. I didn't *have* to shoot the chain, but what other choice could I have made?

Oh, maybe I could bother to learn how to actually work my magic so that if I ever came face to face with Rufus again, I'd actually be able to fight him instead of relying on other folks to save me—which had happened at every possible turn up to this point.

And now a werewolf—a snarling, man-eating creature, was loose in Magnolia Cove.

"Good job, Pepper. Keep up the excellent work," I said to myself.

The trees cleared to a meadow. I swooped down, no idea what I was going to do. I kicked into high speed and nearly caught up with the wolf.

I figured in a few more minutes the beast would shift into his human form. If I could keep up with it until then, without anyone finding out, then everything would be okay.

But I had to stay on its heels.

The sun didn't have too much farther to go.

The werewolf raced on. We were still in the meadow. I pushed my skillet farther, close to the ground.

It was apparently too close. The tip grazed earth, sending the back of the skillet up into the air—with me still on it.

The world turned topsy-turvy. I didn't know which way was up and which was down until my back hit the ground.

The wind knocked from my lungs and I lay on the grass, sucking in air like a fish out of water. Something poked my back and I realized it was the shotgun.

And then growling filled my ears. I shivered, mostly from fear and not the wet grass soaking into me.

I tipped my head back. There, maybe twenty feet and only one or two leaps away, stood the beast.

He snarled and growled, shifting right and left. If I made the move to grab the gun, he would pounce. I could feel it.

"Stop," I said. "I didn't shoot you when I could have. I didn't harm you. There's no need for you to harm me."

Saliva dripped from its jaws. The creature sank onto its haunches as if about to launch itself toward me. I moved to grab the shotgun as daylight cracked across the sky.

And the creature shrank. The fur dissolved from its skin, the muscles contorted, diminishing and erasing. The bones popped as they reconstructed into a human form. To be honest, I couldn't take my eyes away.

It was kinda like watching a car accident—or being a gaper driving past an accident after it's happened. I just had to keep watching.

So I did, y'all—I ain't ashamed to say it.

I watched, holding my breath until what was left of the beast had vanished, and in its place stood the form of a perfectly naked man.

Yes, naked.

The collar hung around his neck, the broken end of it dangling on his chest. Dark hair hung to his shoulders and his blue eyes pierced my heart, sending a shudder straight to my core.

Axel's gaze dragged over me from foot to head. "So now you know what I am. I'm a werewolf, the most dangerous creature in all of Magnolia Cove and if the sun hadn't come up just now, I would've killed you."

SEVENTEEN

*W*e sat in Axel's kitchen. What was it with me seeing naked men this week? Crap! I'd forgotten all about helping Mayor Potion this morning. Hopefully, Grandma had dealt with it. Otherwise, this town was about to have a heart attack—their werewolf had run free (luckily no one knew) and their mayor was a drunk who wound up naked and downtown every morning.

Sheesh. What a town Magnolia Cove was turning out to be.

Axel had showered, dressed and was making a pot of coffee in his express Bunn machine. He dropped in some grounds, pressed a button and in about two seconds had a full pot of coffee.

Wow. It was like a miracle or something.

He was now also fully dressed in a long-sleeved black rib-hugging t-shirt and jeans that hung low on his hips.

I nearly drooled onto the chair next to me.

And yes, I did see him in the buff, but I tried really hard not to look and all I'll say is he's seriously built.

Axel slid a cup of coffee over to me. I picked it up and inhaled deeply. "Thanks."

We both sipped our coffee. I cringed at the bitterness. Axel's blue eyes dragged from my face. He reached for a glass jar and uncapped it. He pushed it over. Filled to the brim were colorful jelly beans.

"What?" I said.

He shrugged. "I thought you might like them."

My heart fluttered up to my mouth. I swallowed it as I tossed a few jelly beans in my cup. I stirred them in and drank.

"Better," I said.

"You're the only person I've ever met who sweetens drinks with jelly beans."

I flashed him a bright smile. "You're the only person I've met who keeps them around for me."

His smile tightened as if I'd said something I shouldn't. "Do you need to call Betty or your cousins?"

I cringed. "Yes! I left my phone in the forest."

He handed me his. "Here you go."

I texted Amelia. *I'm fine. Werewolf is contained. I'll explain everything later.*

A minute passed before his phone dinged. It was Amelia. *Whose phone are you texting from?*

I didn't know what to say. *I'll explain but I'm okay.*

Axel came around the counter and sat in the chair next to me. His clean scent of pine trickled up my nose. His hair was slowly drying. The ends curled as the air hit it.

"So now you know," he said, not looking at me.

"And knowing is half the battle."

He smirked. I had the feeling he wasn't in the mood for jokes. "This isn't GI Joe. This is real life."

I squirmed a little, not sure what to do, but then I tossed my hair back and figured, what the heck? Life is about living—I wasn't going to let this little hiccup freak me out.

"You kissed me yesterday," I said.

Axel raked his fingers through his hair. "I was going to tell you today. It wasn't fair of me to keep it from you. But the way you found out—I didn't want that, either. I didn't want you to fear me."

I shook my head. "I'm not afraid of you."

His gaze dropped to the floor. "Pepper, I saw the look in your eyes when you realized it was me. You were horrified."

"That's a strong word."

"But it's the right one."

I inhaled a deep shot of air. "It's not every day I see a werewolf shift, okay? It was surprising. But back in the hedges, after Rufus showed up, I looked at you and you didn't attack me."

His eyes narrowed. "Rufus attacked you?"

I gnawed the inside of my lip. "You don't remember?"

He shook his head. "I don't remember anything when I'm in that state. That's why Betty guards me. I can't be trusted, Pepper. Not when I'm like that. I can't be trusted around anyone. It doesn't matter who they are."

I reached out and stroked his arm. He flinched. I pressed my fingers to him again. "That's what I'm trying to tell you. Something registered in your brain when I aimed the gun at you. You either realized it was me or you knew danger when you saw it, because you ran away."

His blue eyes darkened with anger. "And you followed me?"

"Well, yeah. I had to make sure you weren't going to hurt anyone."

He sank back in his chair. "And that's the truth of it. I get locked up on full moons because I'm a danger to people."

"How long does the full moon last?"

"For me, only one night. But when you look in the sky you'll think about 3 nights."

"That's only one night a month that you're a werewolf."

"Sometimes two. When there's a blue moon."

I rolled my eyes. "Are you serious? Rufus is out there playing vampire on people and you've got a complex about turning into a werewolf twelve times a year? I think you're making this a bigger issue than it really is."

His jaw twitched as he shook his head. "You don't know what it's like."

I shrugged. "I know what a lot of things are like. I know what being irresponsible is like. I know what losing a loved one is like. I even know what putting your trust in the wrong person feels like. I know all those things and from the little I know about you, I believe that you're one of the good guys. Someone worth putting faith in. Someone who's not going to let me down unless it's unavoidable, and someone who wouldn't normally hurt me. You know when you shift. You can look it up on your phone, for Pete's sake. So what are you getting your panties all up in a wad about?"

Axel got off the stool and crossed to a window. He glanced out. Sunshine splashed across his face. The crinkles next to his eyes pinched as he stared out.

"People judge me."

"People judge all of us. You live in the South. If you don't go to church people either judge you or they try to get you to go with them. Some of the staunchest folks in that church will condemn you to an eternity in brimstone and fire if you don't live the right way. Are you telling me that you, Axel Reign, private investigator and werewolf, are a little freaked out by what other people think?"

He shook his head. "No. I don't care about them. I care about you."

"You have a funny way of showing it. You've barely been around since Todd Turnkey tried to kill me."

"Not by choice."

Todd Turnkey was a past police officer in town who had killed his uncle, Ebenezer Goldmiser, though I had been suspected of the murder.

As if.

I didn't go around killing people.

I folded my arms. "By what then if not by your own choice? Some fear that I'll discover you're a big bad werewolf who's going to kill me? You saved me tonight. If it hadn't been for you, Rufus would've killed me. Or done whatever it is he wants with me— weird squirrelly guy that he is."

He pressed the heels of his hands to his eyes. "I was going to tell you anyway. I made that decision when I kissed you."

I clicked my tongue. "Then what are we arguing about?"

He turned to me. Deep, dark pain that must've been nearly as old as he was shone in his gaze. "People fear what they don't understand, so they fear me. That's why I sit at a table way in the back of the Spellin' Skillet, to keep people from walking out."

I smiled at him. "If they knew you, they wouldn't walk out at all. I'm not trying to blow sunshine up your butt or anything, but if it weren't for you, we never would've found the cat that helped us solve Ebenezer Goldmiser's murder. If it weren't for you, I wouldn't have known that my powers can cause me serious harm if I don't use them every once in a while. If it weren't for you—well, I wouldn't have experienced that awesome kiss yesterday."

His mouth ticked up a bit, curling into a crooked smile.

"You're not an evil monster, and whoever told you that wasn't your friend. I'm your friend and I can see that you aren't. So I think you should take that as gospel truth. Oh, and you're welcome."

He chuckled. "You know what I like about you?"

"No, and I really think you need to tell me because I've blown my hand by telling you what I think of you."

He slowly crossed to me. Axel slid his fingers down my arms and took my hands. I stared into the shining blue ocean of his eyes. "I think you're kind and brave."

I pulled back, laughing. "You're kidding, right? Me, brave?"

"You're a fool if you don't see that. You came to Magnolia Cove not knowing anyone. You embraced your shop and sneaked around trying to figure out who was a killer."

I shifted uncomfortably. "I might call that more stupid than brave."

His eyes twinkled. "Ah, I see. You can give a compliment, but you can't take one."

I bristled. "I can take a compliment."

"Then take the one I just gave you."

"Fine. Thank you for saying all those nice things about me."

He squeezed my hands. "There you go."

"Even if they're not exactly true."

"Buzzkill. Right there."

Our gazes locked and we both laughed. He pulled me to him, wrapping me in a giant bear hug. Heat from his body wafted into me, warming me to the bone. I sighed. He drew away and brushed a strand of hair from my eyes. He dipped his head and our lips met. Sweet, hot fire spread along my neck, sending a tingle filtering through my body.

I wanted to give in to it. Let him kiss me forever, but I was determined to keep my head screwed on straight and do everything I could exactly right. Magnolia Cove was my chance to start over.

When our lips parted, I said, "I accept what you are. It doesn't bother me. At all. I don't want you to doubt that."

He nodded. "I know you just got out of something. How about we go slow?"

"And how about if you have any more deep dark secrets, you trust me. I don't judge books by their covers."

He nodded. "When I start eating baby goats I'll let you know."

I poked his ribs. "That's gross."

He shrugged. "It's what most folks think."

I shot him a flirty smile. "I'm not most folks."

Axel rested his hands behind him on the low countertop. He dragged his gaze over me. Heat blazed in his eyes, making my stomach quiver. "You, Pepper Dunn, aren't like anyone I've ever met before."

Since I wasn't interested in becoming a puddle of mush on his floor, I cocked my chin and said, "And I've never met a werewolf before, either. But I sure do like the way you kiss."

He chuckled. "Come on. Let's get you home."

I stuffed my cast iron riding skillet in Axel's truck, as it wouldn't fit in the Mustang. We rolled through town and arrived at Betty's house a few minutes later.

Axel shut off the engine. "Wait."

He got out, crossed to my side and opened the door. "Thank you," I said.

We climbed the steps and entered the house. Betty sat in her rocker, facing the door. "Well, I see someone's been kissing again."

My face flushed.

"And I also see you discovered who the town werewolf is."

"She knows," Axel confirmed.

Betty spat into the fire. It hissed and crackled. Geez. I just realized that woman ran a fire no matter what time of year it was. Right now, it was late summer and she'd been running that thing ever since I arrived. But miraculously, it didn't heat the house to inferno degrees.

"It's probably best that she found out," Betty said.

"Were Amelia and Cordelia very worried?" I said. "I sent Amelia a text."

"They were. When they came to and couldn't find hide nor hair of you, they called me. 'Course, I didn't know where you were, but then Amelia said she'd heard from you." She gave me a hard look. "You broke the only rule."

"Rufus showed up. Tried to take me."

Her eyes flared. "Well, he should be gone now. The spell that allowed him to enter finished."

"But that's twice he came to me yesterday," I said. "He was supposed to be under surveillance."

Betty frowned. "Somebody probably fell asleep on the job. Or he gave them the slip."

Axel shook his head. "No one was supposed to sleep. Extra precautions were supposed to be set."

"Rufus got by them," I said. I rubbed my arms. "Do you think he'll be able to sneak in?"

Axel shook his head. "No. Several witches created the original spell. No way."

I nodded. "That makes me feel safer."

"But now," Betty said, "we've got other things to worry about."

Fear spiked down my spine. "What?"

Betty smacked her lips and said, "Your aunts called."

"So early?"

Betty shook her head. "No. They called last night."

"What is it? Is everything okay?"

"No everything's not okay. They need you."

I cringed. What could they possibly need me for? Everywhere they went, trouble ensued. At first, I thought my grandmother and cousins were exaggerating, but now I knew they were right.

I fiddled with the collar of my shirt. "What could they possibly need me for?"

Betty's hard stare made my knees liquify. "They want to take you shopping."

EIGHTEEN

*M*int and Licky picked me up at ten am. On the dot.
Which scared me a little. Weren't they supposed to be
late and irresponsible?

Apparently not when it came to taking their favorite new-in-town
niece out for some fresh clothes and witchy things.

Since it was Tuesday, Familiar Place was closed, as were a few
other shops, though some bucked the regular off day and opened.

"We wanted to apologize for getting you in trouble with Leona,"
Mint said.

"It wasn't nice of us to make you get our food without telling the
truth," Licky said.

"You got that right," I grumbled.

Mint put her hands on my shoulders. "Anyway, we're going to take
you to one of our favorite stores in town. It's over by Spellin' Skillet."

"What is it?" I said.

Licky waved her hand dismissively. "Oh, you'll love it."

The fact that they didn't answer my question didn't give me much
confidence. But I was willing to try anything once. I got on my skillet
and followed them as we flew over the trees and houses of downtown,
landing by the Spellin' Skillet a few minutes later.

I'd been over here a few times, and the words over the restaurant took so much of my attention, I hadn't really noticed the fact that a couple of other stores were perched right beside it. The wooden porch wrapped over to the neighbor shops and the purple awning drooped, creating a cover.

"Witch's Wardrobe. So what do they sell?"

Licky squeezed my hand. "Everything. Even wands."

"Wands? Do people use those?"

Mint tossed her long hair over one shoulder. "Some do. Come on."

We entered the store. The inside was an explosion of color. There were tops and gowns, pants and skirts in all hues and patterns. Shoes and striped socks, pointy hats and attachable bat's wings for when you felt like looking like a bat, I suppose. Everything top to bottom was either something a witch wore to look more like a witch, or it was perfectly normal so that you could fit into regular society.

"Well, I declare," came a voice from my right. "If it isn't the new familiar matcher—Pepper Dunn."

I glanced into the smiling face of Idie Claire Hawker, the town's local hair stylist and gossip. "Hey there, Idie," I said.

Idie fluffed her mountain of teased and sprayed hair. "Hey, yourself. I see you've brought your wonderful aunts. Hey, Mint! Hey, Licky!"

My aunts waved as they scrolled through the racks of clothing.

Idie sidled up to me. "Watch it with those two," she said. "They're trouble."

I stifled a laugh. "You don't have to tell me. They've already gotten me into a heap with Leona Doodle."

Idie's mouth puckered into an *o*. "Really?" She glanced from side to side to make sure no one was listening. "Well, from what I've heard, Leona has her own troubles."

I frowned. "What do you mean?"

"Well, you know the festival is still going on, except not as bright as it normally is because of Melbalean's death."

"Sure," I said.

"From what I understand, last night Leona acted really strangely. She attacked some people."

I shrugged. "I mean, she almost attacked me when she found out I was buying food for my aunts. Apparently, they're on some Do Not Serve list."

Idie swallowed. "That's not what I mean. What I'm saying is it was a full-fledged attack. Like she went after them with a spatula and had to be pulled off a man."

I tapped my lip. "Wow. That is weird."

She leaned forward. "Just between you and me, they're saying she went feral."

I frowned. "Feral?"

"Umm-hmm." She smiled brightly. "Anyway, come in and see me sometime. I'd love to get my hands on that beautiful hair of yours. Give you a little snip snip and style it a bit. You have gorgeous locks."

"Thanks," I said. I waved as she left.

There was something strange about what she said. Leona had gone feral. A chicken had attacked Betty, Melbalean had been slashed to death, and even the birds at my store had attacked Rufus in almost a feral, unhinged manner.

There was something there, but I wasn't sure what.

Mint grabbed my arm. "There's something we want to show you."

"It's the reason we came here," Licky said.

They dragged me to the back of the store where a seven-foot-tall oak wardrobe stood open. In it hung a black dress with sharp scalloped edges, making it look like a true witch outfit for Halloween.

"What's that?" I said.

"This," Mint said with authority, "is what's called a Flutter Dress."

I quirked a brow. "Never heard of such a thing. Does it talk?"

Licky trilled a light laugh. "No, sweetheart. It helps you do things. Like if you're going to a dance, you'd wear this dress or another one with the same magic, and wear it. The gown would help you be a better dancer."

I pinched the material and slid my fingers down it. "It's light and soft."

"I design them that way," came a voice.

I glanced in the wardrobe's mirror. A tall woman with flowing black hair and a black suit strode forward. "I'm Gretchen Gargoyle and I'm a sewing witch. This is my store."

"Your clothes are beautiful."

She smiled. "You should try on a Flutter Dress. Let me find one that suits you in color." She eyed the line and said, "You need a robin's egg blue. I think there is one in back. Let me get it."

When she disappeared, Licky thrust the black one in my arms. "Try this one on while she looks. You can at least see what it's like."

I found the dressing room and slipped from my clothes. The soft cotton felt like silk as it slid over my hips. I threaded my hands through the arms and sashayed from side to side, admiring the image in the mirror.

The dress hugged my curves, accentuating what was there. The black was a little harsh for my pale skin and it made the freckles on my nose seem even darker and my brown eyes nearly looked black, but it was a cool gown.

I opened the dressing room door and twirled for Mint and Licky.

Licky clapped her hands. "Beautiful."

Mint smiled. "Really gorgeous. You need to get one."

I nodded. "It's nice, but how does the power work?"

Licky snapped her fingers. "Simple. Think about something you're either not very good at or uncomfortable doing and try to do it. What's something you don't have much experience with?"

I shrugged. "Well, you said it earlier—I've never really danced."

"Okay," Mint said. "So think about dancing and start twirling."

I cracked my knuckles. I would feel like a Grade-A-Idiot for dancing in front of these two.

"It'll be fine," Licky said, as if reading my mind. "No one judges here. Just try."

I swallowed a ball of nerves in my throat and thought about dancing.

Then it started.

My hips swung. My feet swept across the parquet floor. My arms flailed as my body jutted forward.

"Just go with it," Licky said. "You'll see."

So I did. I let the dress twirl and salsa me back and forth. My feet nearly flew out from under me as I struggled to keep up.

"Okay," I said, grinning, though I'm pretty sure I looked more like I was grimacing than anything else. "I'm ready to stop."

"Just tell it," Mint said. "It'll calm down for you."

I focused on stopping but the dress did the exact opposite. It sped up. I threw my arms out in front of me to keep from hitting a cabinet full of clothes. My feet scrambled and my spine snapped as my feet kicked into gear.

"Something's wrong," I said. "Get Gretchen."

Licky grimaced. "I hope it's not us."

"I'm pretty sure it is," I snarled. "It's your curse!"

Gretchen must've heard the commotion because she raced into the room. "Oh no! Be careful. Don't rip the dress. It's one of a kind."

"I'm trying to stop," I yelled. "But it's not helping."

"Try harder," Mint yelled.

Thanks. What exactly did they think I was doing? I was trying. I had focused on stopping and halting, but nothing was working.

An idea flared. If thinking about stopping didn't work, what if I did the opposite? What if I told the gown to speed up, give it everything it had?

I felt a sudden tug in one direction, then the same tug in another. It was like the dress was pulling itself two different ways. I heard a *screech* as seams started ripping.

"Please don't tear it," Gretchen said, clutching the ends of her hair.

I pushed harder, commanding the gown to do more, work harder.

The fabric hummed against my body. I tugged at it, trying to get it off, but it was stuck. The darned thing wouldn't budge. Meanwhile, I was still moving, though not as much as before. Gretchen rushed to me. She started to pull the gown over my head but it wouldn't move.

Mint and Licky tried, too, but the fabric was plastered to me.

At that moment, the dress shot me out from the circle of women.

Okay. I'd had enough. It was time to end this.

I focused everything I had on pushing the dress to its limits. I felt a buildup of energy in my head, like a fist pressing against my brain. I pushed harder until a loud *RIIIIP* filled the store. The gown fell from my body, leaving me in my underwear.

But the magic I'd used had been too much. At the exact same time, every stitch of clothing fell from all the racks and shelves, spilling onto the floor.

Licky grimaced. "Well, I guess that's one way to get it off."

Mint nodded. "Could've been worse, y'all. Could've been worse."

I glanced at Gretchen, who had turned a deep shade of red. She opened her mouth and screamed, "Get out! If I see y'all in this store again, I will personally kick you in the rear end so hard you'll end up in China!"

Well, that was one way to make an exit.

NINETEEN

*N*eedless to say, I had pretty much decided never to shop with Licky and Mint again. Ever. I was also a thousand and one percent sure that they were chaos witches.

I tugged on my clothes, we said our goodbyes and I headed to the house.

Betty laughed when she saw me. "I tried to warn you."

I frowned. "No, you didn't. You let me go. I was kicked out of a shop thanks to those two. Not sure my reputation will be able to rebound."

Betty cackled. "Your reputation will be fine. If Mayor Potion can hide his drunk nakedness, then you'll be okay, too."

I plopped in a chair. "I suppose so…I tell you, I'm beginning to understand why y'all sent Mint and Licky away. They're something else."

Amelia bounded down the stairs. Her hair was long again, but there was something off about it. "Is that?" I squinted. "Is that a wig?"

She rolled her eyes and yanked it off. "Dang. I guess you can tell. Betty still hasn't gotten her full powers back and we can't seem to get my hair to grow."

She tossed the wig on the table and sank onto the couch. "Why,

Grandma? Why would you let this man into my life and then take him away?"

Betty shook her head. "I don't know what you're talking about. Can I help it if the police screwed up my powers?"

Amelia gave her a hard stare. "It wasn't the police. You had a cold."

Betty shook her head. "All right. Let me give it one more shot. But don't you do anything stupid like wash it before you see him."

Amelia perked up. "I won't."

Betty put her corncob pipe in her mouth and covered one nose like St. Nick about to fly up a chimney. Sparks snorted from the pipe and trickled over Amelia. Her golden hair elongated into beautiful wavy locks; her makeup became instantly contoured and she looked absolutely stunning.

The doorbell rang. "Whew," Amelia said, rising, "just under the wire." She crossed to Betty and kissed the top of her silver curls and opened the door.

Lane Longmire stood on the other side. His dark pompadour swooped high like it had the first time I saw him. He flashed a slick grin at Amelia.

"You look beautiful," he said.

She snaked a hand around his elbow. "Thanks."

Lane gave us a wave. "We're off to enjoy the park and the Potion Pools. Anyone care to join us?"

Not interested in being anyone's third wheel, I said, "No thanks."

As soon as the door shut, I turned to Betty. "Do you really think that's a good idea?"

"What?" she said innocently.

"Amelia's being someone she's not for this guy. She doesn't have long hair and she doesn't wear makeup like that."

Betty shrugged. "It's her life. She's got to figure it out."

"Great advice for a grandmother."

Betty stoked the fire. "That's what I thought, too."

"I was being sarcastic."

"Not to me, you weren't."

Cordelia tromped downstairs. She snatched an apple from the

fruit bowl on the table and polished it on her shirt. She unhooked her purse from a peg by the door and slung it over her shoulder.

"Where are you going?" Betty said.

"I've things to do. Sorry. They're important. For work. Anyway, I'll see y'all later."

She escaped quicker than a mouse down a hole, leaving Betty and me staring with blank expressions on our faces.

"She's up to something," Betty said.

I yawned. "Well, I'm exhausted. I need a nap."

I started up the stairs when Betty stopped me. "Do you want to talk about Axel?"

I sighed. "What's there to say? The guy's a werewolf. You seem to think he's okay, so I should, too."

Betty frowned. "There are those who don't like him."

I slid my hand up the railing. "I haven't been in town long enough to care who those people are. After all, I'm the only person who helps witches find their familiars. And if they don't have me—who've they got?"

Betty laughed a hearty bellyful. "Spoken like one of my offspring."

I sealed my lips as I had no idea what to say in reply. I climbed the stairs and collapsed on my bed. Mattie jumped off the window seat and hopped up next to me. I gave her a good stroke right as my phone rang.

I fished it from my pocket and glanced at the screen. Axel's name flashed.

"It's Axel," I said, figuring Mattie couldn't read. "Should I answer it? Or should I play hard to get?"

"Sugarbear, it might be about business and not about kissin'."

"Good point." I thumbed it on. "Hello?"

"Hey," he said in the husky voice of his. My insides quivered. "It's Axel."

"Hey," I said.

"So I got some news about the chickens."

I pressed myself up. "You do? That's great. What've you found out?"

The sound muffled for a moment as if he were switching ears. "I called the company about Melbalean's and Betty's chickens and they didn't have their addresses on file."

"What? How is that possible?"

"That's what I wondered. The guy said he'd need the serial numbers from the boxes, so I tracked one of the numbers from Garrick."

I twisted the comforter absently between my fingers. "And he gave it to you?"

"Yeah. It's a lead he's not pursuing. He's still looking for a killer with a knife."

"So am I," I said.

"Well, that's where this gets interesting," Axel said.

"Tell me more," I said.

He cleared his throat. "I gave the guy the serial number from one of the boxes and he said that chicken wasn't shipped here. It was shipped to a town called Hollyhock Hollow."

I kicked off my shoes and said, "I just heard about it the other day."

"It's another witch town, but it's not as cool as this one."

I laughed. Was he flirting? Yes, I think he was. I started to twirl a strand of hair around my finger but then I realized that first of all, Axel wasn't in here, and second of all, we were talking about murder and flirting wasn't really what I needed to be doing, either.

I cleared my throat in a very professional sounding way. "Okay. So it's another town. What does all this mean?"

Axel's voice hardened. "What I think it means is that someone from Hollyhock Hollow ordered those chickens and sent them on to Betty and Melbalean."

I frowned. "But how? First, they would've had to know that Betty and Melbalean were going to order them, wouldn't they?"

"You said yourself you heard that Melbalean had spied on Betty. What if someone was spying on Melbalean?"

"But then wouldn't they have just sent one to Melbalean? Why include Betty?"

Axel paused. "If you had an opportunity to get back at someone and you were putting all your faith in a chicken, would you just want one chicken, or would you want to increase your odds by having two chickens involved?"

I grabbed a brush and started working it down my tresses. It snagged on a tangle until I ripped the tines through. "I guess I'd want two chickens, but we're talking about chickens, here. It's not like we're talking about assassins."

Axel paused.

"You think we're talking about chicken assassins?" I said.

"A murder weapon wasn't found, but a chicken covered in blood was. That chicken pointed the finger at Betty. You said you tried talking to Betty's chicken earlier in the day and the bird didn't have enough brains for conversation."

"Yeah, but…"

Well, yeah but what? I'd originally stated that it was a ludicrous idea that a chicken could commit murder, but what if it was so ludicrous that someone had taken advantage of the idea and turned it into reality?

Was it possible?

"Okay," I said, "say someone did turn a chicken into the ultimate killing machine, and that's what got Melbalean. How do we prove it? The police have both chickens, all we have is the name of a town where the chickens were re-routed through."

"Hollyhock Hollow is pretty small," he said. "Around the size of Magnolia Cove."

"Okay," I said.

"You want to have dinner tonight?" he said.

I frowned. "You were talking about Magnolia Cove. Not about dinner with me."

"I thought you might like to have a real date."

"You mean finding you naked in the middle of a meadow doesn't count? You did make me coffee afterward."

"You're very cheeky."

"I saw some cheek on you."

He didn't say anything. Had I gone too far?

"I'm kidding. I didn't see any cheek. I didn't look. It wasn't polite."

When he spoke, Axel's voice was low. "I was actually hoping you'd seen both cheeks."

I laughed. "Okay. Maybe I did. But you were asking about dinner. What do you have in mind?"

"There's a steakhouse in Magnolia Cove. White tablecloth. Lots of out-of-towners go there. We could head over and then maybe go to Lightning Bug Creek."

"Lightning Bug Creek?"

"Yeah. It's pretty cool. You'd have to see it to believe it."

"Okay, sure. But I think you were telling me about who lived in Hollyhock Hollow."

"Yeah," Axel said. "I was. Okay, so there are two people among the residents of Hollyhock Hollow with strong connections to Magnolia Cove. The first is Leona Doodle."

My eyebrows shot to peaks. "The restaurant owner?"

"One and the same," he said.

I mused on that for a second. "I don't know anything about her, but it's possible anyone could have a grudge against Melbalean."

"Exactly," Axel said. "Melbalean kept her extracurricular activities a secret from us, but plenty of people knew about them."

Which gave me an idea. Leona was still in town and would be for at least another day or so—which is when the festival concluded. These folks in Magnolia Cove were serious about their festivals. They didn't just last a weekend. They went on for nearly a week, murder or no murder.

"Okay, so Leona. Who's the other person from the town?"

"This one took more digging to find out, but I eventually figured it out. First name Robert, last name Longmire."

I paused. "I don't know a Robert Longmire. The only Longmire I know is Lane, the guy who's dating Amelia."

"Right," Axel said. "Robert Longmire was born about the same time as Lane. At least the birthday looked about right to me. Doing more digging, I came across the man's entire name—Robert Lane Longmire."

AMY BOYLES

I gasped. "So it is Lane Longmire. That family has a beef with Melbalean. Supposedly she cursed them so that they don't live past thirty."

"I thought it was webbed feet," Axel said.

"It's not. It's a longevity issue," I said.

"Mm. I told you that guy was lying about something the night we found him snooping around the festival supposedly looking for more flowers."

"But what could he have been looking for?" I said.

"His hair," Axel joked.

I laughed. "He's grown that back. Betty made sure of it. So if he came here to kill Melbalean and break his family's curse, what's he still doing here?"

"I don't know, but I have a feeling that if Melbalean did curse the Longmires, her death would've broken that."

"What about the face in the egg?"

"A curse is different than stealing someone's attribute. Melbalean's death wouldn't have broken that sort of spell. That's different magic. Either way, we need to find out why he's still in town. My guess it's not just about your cousin."

"We?" I said. "You accept that I'm helping you on this?"

"I don't mean 'we' in that sense."

My heart deflated a little.

"But I do need your help."

"Why?"

He cleared his throat. "Because after doing a little more digging, I found out that Lane is taking Amelia to a very nice restaurant tonight."

"Let me guess, the steakhouse."

"Right," Axel said. "And you and I are also going there."

I bristled. "I thought it was a date."

He chuckled. "It is a date. We're going, but there's something we need to do."

I folded one arm over the other, almost a little hurt that my date night with the werewolf I practically drooled for, was now a working dinner. "What is it we need to do?"

Axel's voice turned into a low growl. "We need to spy on Lane. Find out what he's up to."

And in that one moment, the surge of adrenaline that flowed through me at the thought of spying on Amelia's boyfriend made everything all right.

TWENTY

I did manage a short nap and time to feed and water the animals at Familiar Place before I had to get ready for dinner. Amelia returned from her date in the park with Lane and got ready for her dinner. I heard Lane pick her up as I was applying the finishing touches to my makeup.

The doorbell rang again and I met Cordelia in the hallway. She was dressed in leather pants and a long-sleeved silver shirt. My eyes flared when I saw her.

"Do you have a date?"

She laughed nervously. "No. No. I have a boyfriend. Zach, remember? I don't have a date."

"You sure do look dressed for one," I said.

She scoffed. "No. I'm not dressed for a date. Definitely not."

"Okay," I mumbled, "but you look kinda dressed for a date."

She shot me a look so scathing I hid my smile behind my hand, because I had to be right. We each headed downstairs. Me for a date with Axel and Cordelia not for a date.

Betty opened the door. Axel stood there. He wore a black blazer over a black v-neck tee and black jeans. His hair hung around his massive shoulders and a wonderful spicy scent wafted off him.

My heart thrummed in my throat. "Hi," I said.

His blue eyes sparkled. "Hi."

I turned to my family. "Well, we'll be off. Should be home later, maybe before Cordelia returns from her date."

She glared at me.

Betty stirred something in the cauldron. She raised the spoon and wagged it at me. "I've got my strength and magic back. You'd better be home by curfew, kid. I don't want to have to look for you."

I did my best not to roll my eyes and I headed out with Axel. I slid into the seat of his Mustang and twisted my fingers together, as hormones ripped through me. All I wanted to do was knot my fingers into his hair and kiss him.

I licked my lips and bit the inside of my mouth to calm down.

"So what's the plan?" I said when he slid in next to me.

His gaze raked over me like blazing coals. He glanced away quickly, focusing on the road. He pulled out into the street and I settled into the bucket seat.

Even though all I wanted to do was kiss him.

Really, Pepper. I need to go slow. Take my time.

I mean, I knew Axel was a werewolf, but it's not like I knew much else about him.

"I was chased here," Axel said.

Well, it looked like I was about to find out quite a bit.

"I'd been to Magnolia Cove several times when I was young. My parents loved coming here. They're a mixed couple. Mom's a witch and Dad's a werewolf. It's not a traditional arrangement. Witches and werewolves, for the most part, do not get along. They each stay with their own kind. It's made it hard for me, trying to figure out where to fit in. I was living up North outside Chicago, working as a private investigator in a witch community. From what I can figure, one of the local wolf packs wanted to increase their territory, so they attacked the witch's animals."

He inhaled deeply. "I had the same trouble there as I do here. A lot of folks don't trust me. Just because of what I am. I was accused of the slaughter and attacked. I had to run, but they followed—all the way here."

He steered with one hand, rotating the wheel as we wound through the curving streets. "A lot of people remembered my parents and me from when I was little, so they let me stay. Helped me. The witches backed off but I was told never to return there. That wasn't a problem. I don't intend to ever go back."

Pain sliced across his face. To be accused of a crime and hunted like an animal must've been horrible—awful. I wanted to fold my arms around Axel and hug him.

"What about your parents?" I said.

"They live in an RV and are traveling the countryside. They're in the Rockies right now. I talk to them every week, but I didn't want to involve them in that."

We pulled up to a restaurant made of stacked stone and dark glass. He killed the engine and turned to me. "I wanted you to know before we walked in here."

I nodded. "Okay."

He came around and opened my door. I took his hand. It was warm and the electricity between us sent a jolt to my core. I swallowed the knot in my throat, and suddenly feeling very shy, I turned to glance at the restaurant.

"Shall we?" he said.

"We shall."

We entered to several glances. A couple of people scowled when they saw us, but nothing crazy happened.

I gazed around the dining room until I saw Amelia and Lane. Her eyes locked on mine and I waved. The table right beside theirs was empty.

"Oh," I said to the hostess as I pointed. "We'll sit there."

She grabbed a couple of menus and led us toward Amelia and Lane. Axel placed a hand on my back and whispered in my ear, "Good job."

In less than a minute we were seated next to them. I flashed a smile at my cousin. "Imagine seeing you here. What a coincidence. Don't mind us. We won't bother y'all."

Amelia smiled. "No bother at all. We were just saying how this is such a small town."

Lane flashed that thousand-watt smile of his. "We sure were."

Axel slid into a seat parallel to Lane. "You know, I think I know you from somewhere. Aren't you originally from Hollyhock Hollow?"

Lane nodded enthusiastically. "I am. Lived there all my life." He flashed a look to Amelia. "That is, until I started chasing yetis and sometimes dragons."

Axel popped his menu and turned to Lane. "You know, I've heard that dragons are a lot like chickens."

Lane cleared his throat. "Oh. I wouldn't know about that." He shot a grin to Amelia. "I've spent so many years taming the beasts that anything I would've known about chickens to begin with is now long gone in my memory."

Axel smiled. "I can imagine. From just looking at the two creatures, they don't seem to have a lot in common—one breathes fire, the other clucks. But I've heard they have other similarities. The way they roost, for instance."

Lane shrugged. "I wouldn't know."

Axel propped himself up on one elbow. "I had a good childhood friend from Hollyhock. He said on the outskirts of town there were dozens of long chicken houses. Lots of chicken farmers in Hollyhock."

Lane dragged his gaze from Amelia's questioning look and gave Axel a tight smile. "I know a few myself."

Axel glanced at his menu. "Yep. That's what I hear. Lots of chicken farmers."

"You know," I said, leaning over toward Amelia, "no one wants to say it, but I think Melbalean was killed by that chicken."

Amelia frowned. "That's silly. I've never heard of anything like that."

"Oh, I have," Lane said.

We all turned to him. He stared at his menu as he spoke. "My dad once fed a chicken some feed that was supposed to help them grow larger, but instead it made the chicken really angry. Volatile to the point where it started attacking people."

I nodded. "I even heard Leona attacked some customers at the festival. Maybe she's been eating chicken feed."

We all laughed except Amelia, who cocked her chin toward Lane. "I thought you said your dad was a dragon hunter. Y'all hunted together."

Lane's cheeks flushed. "We are. We do. He is. Did I say my dad? I meant my uncle raises chickens."

Her frown deepened. "You said your uncle hunted dragons with y'all, too."

"Did I?" Lane said. His gaze skirted from one side of the dining room to the other. "Wow. Is it getting hot in here?" He sipped his water.

Amelia sat back. "Lane, are you a chicken farmer?"

Lane spewed water from his mouth straight onto Amelia's hair. She shrieked, rising to dab at the moisture.

Lane rose, snatched his napkin and helped blot the water.

"Don't," Amelia said. "I've got it. It's okay."

"I'm so sorry," he said.

One of her strands slid down her arm. Lane took it between his fingers. "Your hair's coming out."

Amelia grabbed it. "Let go of it."

Lane retreated as the water apparently did a reverse spelling on Amelia's locks. In less than ten seconds, the extensions fell to the floor, leaving her with the original, short pixie cut.

Lane's face twisted in horror. "Your hair! It's fake."

Amelia threw down her napkin. "Better my hair be fake than me. You, Lane Longmire, are a chicken farmer claiming to be a dragon hunter. You're a bigger liar than I am."

With that, Amelia huffed from the dining room, leaving the rest of us to watch her go.

I grimaced at Axel. "I'll be right back."

I found Amelia outside beneath a weeping willow. She turned when she heard me and knuckled away a tear.

"He's a liar," she said.

I shrugged. "People rarely tell the whole truth about themselves," I said. "We all want folks to see us in a good light."

"He's a chicken farmer," she croaked. "He's out there chasing chickens, not dragons."

"Too good to be true, huh?"

She nodded. "And the worst of it is that I screamed at my mother, told her I didn't want to see her again because she embarrassed me in front of him." Amelia exhaled a shot of air. "I owe her an apology. Family's important." She glanced at me from under her lashes. "I should be grateful for the family I have."

I rubbed her arm. "I am." I leaned against the tree. "But did you like him? Enjoy spending time with him?"

Amelia nodded.

"Isn't that what matters? Not all this other superficial stuff? I mean, y'all are perfect for each other. He farms chickens. You don't have that much hair—it's a match made in witchy heaven."

She gave me a sly smile. "Sweet tea witchy heaven."

I laughed, thinking of a joke that the three of us had—that we were sweet tea witches, instead of me being a head witch. "What kind of witch are you?" I said.

Amelia rolled her eyes. "It's so boring. I'm an administrative witch. I like to organize things and put them together. That's why I work at town hall. I'm really good at categorizing." She hiccupped a sob. "It's a horrible witch talent, but I can still do other things."

I wrapped my arms around her. "Yes, like be my cousin and friend. Listen, why don't you dry those tears and come in? Who cares about your hair? Amelia, you're beautiful just the way you are. You shouldn't have to change for anyone."

She pressed the heels of her hands to her eyes and inhaled a quivering breath. "You're right. If Lane doesn't like me with short hair, then he's not worth it, is he?"

I shook my head. "He most definitely is not."

Amelia wrapped a hand around my waist. "Thanks for showing up tonight. I needed this."

I gave her a squeeze. "Good. Because there's a reason why Axel and I are here."

She quirked a delicate brow. "Oh? What's that?"

I narrowed my gaze. "We're here to see what else Lane's hiding."

"What do you mean?"

We climbed the steps. "Let's go find out."

We reentered the dining room. Axel had moved to Amelia's spot, apparently consoling Lane, who at this point I thought to be a loser and a swindler, so I had absolutely no problem grilling him about his relationship with Melbalean.

Axel rose when he saw us. "Ladies."

Lane started to rise. "Actually, I might need to get back."

I glared at him. "After what you did to my cousin, you can sit here and answer a few questions."

Lane squirmed in his chair. "Okay."

"You lied about the webbed feet," I said. "That's not the curse Melbalean had put on your family."

He sighed. "No, it's not." He glanced at Amelia. "Most of my family members don't live past thirty."

Amelia frowned. "Your dad's alive."

Lane threaded his fingers through his pompadour. "The men do. The women die early."

Amelia shuddered. "Even the ones who marry in?"

Lane nodded.

Amelia shot me a terrified look. "Glad I know that now."

Lane threw out his hands. "No, I think it's over. Now that Melbalean's dead, I mean. Okay. So I came here to meet you, but I also came to speak with Melbalean, get her to remove the curse."

I quirked a brow. "You did?"

He nodded.

Axel coughed into his hand. "Lane has a sister who's about to turn thirty."

"I do. I came to talk to Melbalean for her. And I did have a chance, but Melbalean wasn't budging. She said the Longmires deserved their curse." He dropped his head into his hands. "I was angry, I'll admit it.

But I didn't kill her. I was going to return, try talking to her again the next day, but as y'all know, she was murdered."

I stared at Lane, saw the sadness and remorse in his face. My heart pinged for his family—his sister and even for him, for the situation he was put in.

He glanced at Amelia. "I'm so sorry I lied, but you have no idea how hard it is to find someone who wants to date a chicken farmer. Women think I smell like chickens."

"You don't," Amelia said.

"I scrubbed hard," he said. "Used lots of soap. That Lava stuff works great."

I grimaced at the thought of a rough green Lava bar. That soap was meant for mechanics and the like. I hated to think what had lived under Lane's fingernails that he needed that soap.

"Lane, thanks for telling us," Axel said.

We finished up dinner, actually taking the time to talk about real things, which I think helped Lane and Amelia come to an understanding. Whether or not they were going to continue seeing each other was another subject, one I didn't know the answer to.

I climbed into Axel's car and smiled at him. "So you knew that Lane was lying about the whole dragon hunting thing."

"Yep. And if he was going to tell one lie, would he tell any others?"

I stared out the window as he wove the Mustang down the hill. "I believe him about Melbalean."

"Me too."

"So where does that leave us?" I said.

We drove in silence for a few minutes until we reached a large pond. Red lights floated beneath the surface. "It leaves us here," Axel said.

The surface of the water glowed. "What's this?"

"Lightning Bug Creek."

"It's a pond."

"Someone made it larger."

I rolled my eyes. "Of course."

He strolled around and opened my door. I slid from the seat and

Axel took my hand. "This is the most romantic place in all of Magnolia Cove."

I quirked a brow. "Are you trying to be romantic?"

His lips curved into a delicious smile. "After I almost killed you last night, I sure am."

I laughed, but the serious glint in his eyes cut me short. "Explain this to me."

"These are magical lightning bugs—they're more like pixies, really. You bother them and they'll come to the surface and bite you."

I cringed. "That's not good."

He chuckled. "They live underwater and light the pond at night."

We found a spot to sit on and I watched in amazement as red lights shot back and forth under the surface of the water. It was like watching shooting stars in a lake. It was awesome.

I rested my head on Axel's shoulder. "No one said a word to you at the restaurant."

"They must've been too taken with your beauty," he murmured.

I giggled. "How very sweet."

He tipped my chin toward his face and kissed me long and deep. My insides soared with delight. Pleasure and warm comfort enveloped me as I sighed into him.

He might be dangerous, but right now Axel was dangerous in all the right ways—ready to protect me at a moment's notice.

We parted and I rested my head on his shoulder. I didn't realize I'd fallen asleep until light cracked the sky and Axel was gently shaking me awake.

"Oh gosh," I said, glancing at my watch. "I missed curfew. Betty's going to kill me."

I jumped off the ground and brushed dirt from my clothes. Every muscle in my body kinked. I was stiff and sore. "I was so tired from not sleeping very much last night that I paid for it by dozing off."

Axel raked his hands through his hair. "I was tired, too. Fell asleep myself. I'll take all the blame."

"She'll probably shoot you," I said over my shoulder.

We reached the car and jumped inside. "It'll be fine," he said.

I cracked my knuckles. "She'll probably throw me out. Great. I'll have to find a new place to live. Ugh."

He flashed me a sympathetic smile. "It was my fault. I'm sorry."

"It's not your fault. I fell asleep, too."

We wound back through the streets as daylight spilled yellows and pinks across downtown. I noticed a figure lying in front of the statue of Amaryllis Snitch.

"That doesn't look like Mayor Potion," I said. "Who is that?"

"Let's go see," Axel said.

We slid to a stop and got out. As we neared, my heart thundered in my chest as I started making out silver curls and a jean jumpsuit.

I brought a trembling hand to my mouth. "Oh my gosh."

Axel broke into a run. He reached the body and turned it over.

There, in the middle of downtown, lay a motionless Betty Craple.

TWENTY-ONE

I reached Betty and bent over. I ran my fingers up to her wrist. "How do I check for a pulse?"

Betty's other hand reached over and slapped me away. "I've got a pulse, kid. Get that hand away from me before you do damage with it."

I drew my hand back. "I'm not going to do any damage with it. I'm not even sure how I *could* do damage. I'm just trying to check your pulse."

Axel pulled Betty to a seated position. "What happened?"

Betty scratched her hair. The silver curled wig shifted forward a bit. "I don't know. Heck, I was coming out here to do my morning chores when I was knocked out. What the heck's wrong with this town? When I catch who did this, I'm going to dance naked in front of them."

I quirked a brow at her in confusion.

"Kid, you do not want to see this body naked."

I nodded. "Okay, I get it. That's enough of a punishment for them."

"Right," Betty said.

"Hey y'all," came a voice.

I glanced up and Mayor Potion, dressed I might add, was striding

148

full speed-walk toward us. "I barely woke myself up this morning. I came out here searching for Betty to make sure she's okay. What's this?"

Axel assisted a less-than-enthusiastic Betty all the way to her feet. "I'm fine," she grumbled. "I don't need your help."

"Let's call it a Southern gentleman thing."

She zipped her mouth shut as Axel brought her to standing. She glared at Peter Potion. "You didn't happen to see anyone else milling around town, did you? I think someone knocked me out."

Peter frowned. He glanced right and left before narrowing his eyes. "In fact, I did see one other person running around outside today."

Betty made a fist. "Who was it?"

Peter glanced down, mumbling. "I can't be sure she's involved, of course. It doesn't seem a thousand percent logical that she would be. Very strange, indeed."

"Can you tell us who it was, mayor?" Axel said.

The mayor drummed his fingers over his lips. Finally, he said, "I saw Leona coming from this way."

Betty's eyes narrowed to tiny slits. "So it's her then. Leona better duck for cover, because when this witch gets mad, I explode."

I raised my eyebrows sharply. "Please don't do that. It sounds messy."

Betty folded her hand. "Figure of speech, kid."

WE RETURNED to the house to decompress. Axel wanted to call the doctor, make sure Betty didn't have anything else wrong with her, but she gave him a solid "no".

"I don't need that man poking at me."

"Maybe your blood pressure fell," Axel said.

She glanced at her shotgun. "I dare you to say that again."

I jumped between them, flaring my arms. "Okay, there's no need to get all defensive. Axel's only trying to help. No one's suggesting you're getting older and having problems that only old people have—like low blood pressure, water in the legs, that sort of thing."

Betty frowned. "How do you know about those things?"

"I once had grandparents, you know," I said. "I remember a little bit of what they went through before they died. Anyway, the real question here is Leona and what we're going to do about it. Today's the last day of the festival. I've got a shop to run and if Leona is behind this whole thing, why did she knock you out? I don't understand that."

Axel leaned one shoulder against the wall. "We first have to talk to her and see if she's the one who ordered the chickens. I'll take that part. See if I can get her to talk."

I nodded. "Okay. Will you call me at work? Let me know what you found out?"

He nodded.

Axel left without giving me a kiss on the cheek or the forehead or the lips for that matter. It wasn't something I wanted to do in front of Betty anyway, since she liked to tease me about it.

Betty snapped her fingers and a fire licked and spat beneath the cauldron. I glanced over and it looked like she was making grits for breakfast.

"Why would Leona have hit you?"

Betty shrugged. "Maybe I got in the way somehow."

"But how?"

She tapped a spoon against the cauldron and hung it on a hook above the fireplace. "Say she did come here for Melbalean. Why is *now* so important? Why not have killed her years before?"

I cracked my knuckles. "Maybe they were going to meet and Melbalean was going to give her something?"

Betty plopped into her rocker. "Maybe. Hard to know since she's dead."

I smirked. "It's as good a theory as any, I suppose. But why attack you? That doesn't make any sense."

Betty rubbed her temples. "Maybe Leona wanted the golden eggs and she saw us with the bag."

I laughed. "Oh, wow. I'd forgotten we'd buried it before they arrested you. But don't you think Leona could've just ordered her own golden-egg-laying hen? I mean she might've sent it to you anyway, according to Axel."

Betty leaned forward. "Really?"

"Yep." I explained what we knew about the hens and how they were shipped from an address in Hollyhock Hollow.

Betty rocked steadily back and forth. "So much to think about. Well, let's hope that boyfriend of yours gets it all figured out."

"He's not my boyfriend."

Betty rolled her eyes. "That why you stayed out with him all night last night?" She jabbed a finger at me. "Don't think I don't know that, because I do. Y'all are lucky you saved me from the rest of the town seeing my humiliation this morning. That's why I'm not going to say anything."

I crossed over and wrapped my arms around her. "You're the best grandmother ever."

She pulled away. "You better get ready for work. Those animals won't wait for you."

I beamed at her as I moved to the stairs. "Actually, they will."

I showered and dressed for the day, putting on a pair of fitted blue jeans and a tunic shirt that I belted at the waist so I wouldn't look shapeless.

Mattie stirred from her post on the window seat. "How 'bout I come with you today, sugar?"

"Sure," I said. "I could use some company."

As soon as I unlocked the doors to Familiar Place, I had a swath of people follow me in. They kept me busy while I helped a little boy find his familiar—which turned out to be a Dachshund puppy we'd just received the previous week. Another older witch needed to find herself a replacement for a frog she'd just lost. I found a nice water turtle to become her new familiar.

Really, it was a completely satisfying job and I loved it.

Mattie the cat talked to the animals, whose chatter filled my mind while I helped customers, flipped through the bills and cleaned surfaces. The cats and dogs liked having another creature around—

151

AMY BOYLES

one from the outside who could tell them what was going on in the world.

"And then the chicken killed her," Mattie said.

"No," barked one of the pups.

"You've got to be kidding," one of the kittens said.

"Cross my heart, sugars," Mattie said.

"Okay, don't give the animals bad ideas about chickens," I said.

Mattie jumped to the floor. "I'm just tellin' them the truth."

"That murder hasn't even been solved yet," I said.

The cat sniffed, stopping at the feed box I'd left in a corner. "What's that?" Mattie said. "Some kind of new litter for me to use."

I laughed. "No. Not litter. It's the chicken feed that came with Betty's hen."

Mattie reared back. "Smells weird. Don't smell like any food I've ever eaten."

"That's because it's a grain," I said. "It's not kibble."

Mattie turned her nose from it and flicked her tail. "I'm just sayin'."

My cell rang. I fished it from my purse. Axel's name flashed on the screen. "Hello?" I said.

"Hey, it's Axel."

"Hey," I said, pretending to sound surprised that it was him.

"I spoke with Leona."

I pressed the phone to my ear to make sure I could hear everything he said loud and clear. "Oh?"

"Yeah. She doesn't seem to know anything."

I shook my head. "Impossible. There's no way. She had to have been the person who ordered the hens."

"Well, she's not talking if it was her. I found her in the kitchen of her food trailer and she was so insulted by my questioning she just about kicked me out."

"Hmm. In your experience what does that mean?"

He sighed. "Either she's guilty or she's not."

"Not helpful."

He chuckled. "I know. I'm going to call Garrick, see if he's got anything new."

152

"Maybe he does since he didn't question Betty again."

"That's what I'm thinking," he said. "I'll catch up with you later."

I hung up the phone. It was just past noon. Lunch time. Hanging on the door was a Be Right Back sign. I fiddled with the phone while I thought.

"Mattie, want to take a walk?" I said.

"You bet your lollipops I do."

"Speaking of lollipops," I said, "I'm short on jelly beans. Want to stop by Carmen's store first?"

"I'm following you," Mattie said.

I flipped the sign, intending to return within half an hour or so. We walked the few steps to Carmen's sweet shop, Marshmallow Magic, and entered.

"Hey there," Carmen said, waving from the counter. "How're y'all today?"

"Great," I said. "I need to get some more jelly beans."

Carmen winked at me. Her long, caramel hair hung around her shoulders. "I've already put aside a bag for you. It's got the new flavors and some of your favorites."

I flashed her a brilliant smile. "You are sent by God. You know, I'm embarrassed to ask. I know we're cousins, but I don't know how."

Carmen tucked a strand of hair behind her ear. "I'm Betty's sister's granddaughter. We're not exactly the closest of cousins, but we're not that far off, either."

"How are you a Craple if you're from Betty's side of the family?"

Carmen's eyes sparkled. "The women keep their last names here. All the women were born Craples and they stay Craples until they die."

"Unless you're me," I said. "Seeing how my mom took on her married name and became a Dunn."

"Unless you're you," she agreed.

"Thank you. I'd been wondering about that."

She laughed. "What else is new?"

"Well, Betty thinks someone knocked her out this morning," I said.

Carmen scoffed. "Is that all? She gets low blood pressure sometimes and faints. It doesn't happen very often, but sometimes. She refuses to see a doctor, but maybe you can talk her into it."

I nodded. "Yeah, maybe. Thanks for the beans."

Carmen waved again as I left. "Anytime."

"Hmm," I said, after we'd left.

"What is it?" Mattie said.

"Carmen says Betty's got low blood pressure, even though she swore she was knocked out."

"That's called vanity, child," Mattie said. "You think Betty's going to admit to being weak in any way?"

I ripped open the cellophane bag and popped a deep orange colored bean into my mouth. Ripe peaches flooded my tongue and I moaned. "Seriously, Carmen knows how to make some delicious jelly beans."

"Hmm hmm," Mattie said.

My brain regained its focus. "But then the mayor said he saw Leona darting around town this morning, looking very suspicious."

"And your point is?"

I sucked my tongue. "I don't know that I have one. It's kind of confusing."

"What are we doing out here, anyway?" Mattie said.

"Oh, we're going to check out Leona."

"Sounds like you're cruisin' for a bruisin', sugarbear. I ain't gonna lie."

I smiled. "Good. I like your honesty."

We marched across the lawn to the last day of the Cotton and Cobwebs festival. I didn't see Mint or Licky around and I figured they'd probably been fired as organizers of the event. To be honest, part of me wanted to fire them as my aunts thanks to the chaos they dished out like nice folks dish out compliments.

But anyway.

I reached Leona's and saw a slow line trickling toward the cash register—mostly out-of-towners.

"I'm surprised so many people are still in town," I said to Mattie.

"Oh, this is a big deal. Lots of people come for the custom clothes you can have made, custom weaponry—all sorts of things."

I glanced around. "I guess I've been busy doing other things and haven't noticed."

I didn't want Leona to see me, and to be honest, I didn't exactly know what I was doing. I guided Mattie around the rear, where extension cords ran from the trailer and several trash cans were filled with black bags. Several steps led up to the trailer, and the back door was opened. I had a great view of Leona and her workers. I could see the kitchen, where several people were cooking and Leona stood taking orders.

"Hey, Leona," one of the cooks called, "is this the cornmeal you want us to use?"

The sour expression on Leona's face nearly made me cower behind Mattie. After all, she'd already kicked me from her line once. If she saw me out back, I hated to think what she'd do. I tucked myself behind a light pole as Leona came around.

"What cornmeal?" she said.

The cook pointed to a box sitting on the floor. "That."

"What in tarnation's got a hold of you? No. That's not cornmeal. That's the stuff I made a pan of bread from and ate right before I went after that man for looking at me cross-eyed. Throw that stuff out. I thought I already told y'all to do that."

"Well where'd it come from then?" the cook asked.

Leona threw up her hands. "How the heck should I know? Stuff just showed up."

She went around the front and the cook loaded the box into her arms. She carried it to the trash bin and dropped it in, box and all. As soon as she returned to the trailer, I eased out from behind the pole, and tucked a strand of hair behind my ear—as if that would make me look less weird if someone saw me hiding.

Mattie followed me to the trashcan, where I glanced inside and got a good long look at what the cook dumped.

"That looks exactly like the chicken feed at the shop," I said.

Mattie jumped up on top of a nearby crate and stuck her nose in. "Smells like it, too."

I nibbled my lip while I put the pieces together. Betty's hen had attacked her right after eating. I saw the same food with Melbalean's hen. The birds at my shop tried to scratch out Rufus's eyes after I fed them some and Leona just said that she'd eaten a pan of it right before attacking that man.

"Oh my gosh," I said.

"What?" Mattie said.

"It *was* the hen that killed Melbalean. It ate the chicken feed and went crazy and killed her."

Mattie glanced at me. "So where'd the feed come from?"

I furrowed my brow hard. "There's only one person I know who could've gotten feed."

"Who's that?" she said.

My voice came out rough. "A chicken farmer who claims innocence."

TWENTY-TWO

"*I* already told you I don't know anything about it," Lane said.

I'd called Axel and he met me at the hotel where Lane was staying. We found him packing up his truck. "I might be a chicken farmer, but I didn't put a spell on feed and distribute it around town, and I sure as heck didn't dose Melbalean's chicken so that it would kill her. Like I said, I came to talk to her. I didn't come to kill her."

"*You* might not have, but the chicken did," I said.

Lane shook his head. "It wasn't me. Like I said."

Axel folded his arms. "Any idea who might've done it?"

Lane laughed. "Could've been anybody. Now if you'll excuse me, I'm on my way out of town."

I almost said—got a dragon to catch? But I bit my tongue super hard so I wouldn't.

Lane lifted one last box into his truck bed. What looked like a large paint bucket dumped. The lid fell off and chicken feed spilled over the bed.

I glanced at Axel. "Looks like the same type that Betty's hen had."

Lane threw up his hands. "All right. So I've got some chicken feed. I was supposed to meet someone who wanted to buy a certain kind.

So I brought it into town. Thing is, the guy didn't show. No one did, but the next day I noticed half the feed was gone. I didn't report it stolen because it's chicken feed. I didn't think it was a big deal —until now."

Axel's jaw clenched. "I need to call this into Garrick. He'll want to talk to you."

Lane slumped onto the bumper. "Who knew this town could be so much trouble?"

I'm guessing that meant things were over for him and Amelia. It was a relationship based on lies, thanks in part to Betty, who'd glammed up my cousin's photo to begin with.

Axel called Garrick, who arrived on the scene to interview Lane. I drifted off to the side. Axel strode up.

"Seems weird that someone would've stolen the seed," I said.

Axel raked strong fingers through his thick hair. "Maybe it's coincidence. Maybe he's just saying that. Garrick'll talk to him, figure it out. But as of now, it looks like he's the closest we've gotten to solving this thing."

I smirked at him. "We?"

His lips coiled into a smile. "That's right. We. Now, what're you going to do with the rest of your day?"

I exhaled a deep shot of air, letting a wad of tension roll away. "I don't know about my day, but I haven't enjoyed one night of this festival and I plan on making that priority number one."

Axel smiled. "I'll see you there."

"BETTY, I suggest you stay away from fixing Amelia up with anyone else ever again," I said as I poured myself a glass of sweet tea.

She pinched her lips into a pout. "Why?"

"Because Lane might've been involved in Melbalean's murder. There are no guarantees, but it's a possibility."

"Not only that," Amelia added, "but trying to keep up with all that hair and makeup wasn't me. I wish it were, but I'm a pixie cut kinda gal. I'll put a dandelion behind my ear, polish my cowboy boots and consider that dressing up. But all the hairspray and contouring? That's not for me."

"Good thing," Cordelia said, "because I didn't want to tell you, but all your contouring made it look like you had a mustache."

Amelia flared her fingers and black snow fell on Cordelia.

"Hey," Cordelia said.

I sat back in shock. "Amelia, that's not like you."

Amelia smiled. "Oh, I know. I know I'm normally all rainbows and sparkles, and I think Lane helped break me out of that."

Cordelia clapped her hands and the black snow evaporated. "I kinda like you a little less naive." She pinched her fingers together. "But only a little less."

I glared at Betty. "And I found out you sometimes faint from low blood pressure. First thing tomorrow, you're going to the doctor. First thing so we can get that stabilized."

Betty hugged her arms. "Bunch of big mouths in this town."

I smiled. "Big mouths who love you."

"I'll spell every one of them to fart flowers if they keep poking their noses in my business."

My cousins and I laughed. "Okay. Who's ready to go the festival?"

The last night of the festival was loud and bright. Colored orbs of light floated along the paths and people were dressed in their most vibrant and best witchy gowns.

I felt pretty underdressed in my jeans and short-sleeved tee. But whatever, I was new in town and folks could accept it or not.

Cordelia stepped up beside me. "How was your date the other night?" I said.

"Shh," she said. "No one knows about it."

I twisted my fingers. "So you admit it."

A sly smile curled on her lips. "I'm not saying anything. So can you please keep this between us. Just for now?"

I nodded. "Sure. It's our secret."

She grabbed my hand. "Great. Come on. There's this fun game on the other side of the lawn. It consists of balls of fire. You can only play it on the last night of the festival."

The hair on my nape rose. "Is it dangerous?"

She shrugged. "Maybe a little. That's why it's only one night."

I glanced around and saw Mint and Licky standing on the other side of the lawn, arguing about something. I thumbed toward them. "Well, as long as you keep those two far, far away from the game, everyone should come out alive."

Cordelia looked over her shoulder. "Come on, Amelia. We're going to play Fireballs."

"I'm in," Amelia said.

Fireballs? Definitely sounded dangerous.

It was. You had to control the balls with your magic so they wouldn't set anything on fire or hurt the game barker. I actually found that it was something I could do, which gave me a boost of confidence in the magic department.

"You're pretty good at that," a husky voice whispered beside me.

I aimed my ear toward Axel's mouth, hoping he'd nuzzle it, but instead, he leaned forward and pressed his cheek to mine. A knot of butterflies invaded my stomach at his touch.

"I'm working hard at it," I said about the game. "What've you been up to?"

"Just trying to catch a killer, or figure out who killed Melbalean. All in a day's work."

I turned around and found myself lip to lip with Axel. The world evaporated as I drank in the blue of his eyes.

"Want to go for a walk?" he said.

I nodded as my throat had gone completely dry. "Sure," I croaked.

"You okay?" he said.

I cleared the cobwebs from my voice box. "Yes."

We strolled down a walkway where colored orbs bobbed and twirled. Several other couples had taken the same path.

"It's a beautiful night," Axel said.

"It is."

"It's not as lovely as you, however."

I felt heat ping my cheeks. "I bet you say that to all the girls. After all, you do have the nickname Mr. Sexy."

He laughed. "That's a ridiculous label. I'm a one gal kind of man. When I know who I want."

My heart slammed into my throat. "Oh," I croaked.

He paused and turned toward me. I pivoted to him and felt heat waft from his chest. "I'd like to spend more time with you."

"I thought you'd already said that."

He shook his head. "I haven't said that explicitly. I've said you should stay away from me."

I clicked my tongue. "Oh, that's right. I gave you a thousand reasons why you shouldn't care what other people think."

He brushed a strand of hair from my eyes. "And you know what?" he said in a drawl that made my knees quake.

"What?" I said hoarsely.

"You are right, Miss Lady. You're absolutely right. I'm willing to try, if you are."

I pretended to think about it for a minute. I cocked one eye at him. "Try what, exactly?"

"Admitting to ourselves that it means more than nothing. When we do this."

His lips touched mine and fire razed to my toes. I shivered as he pulled away. "I guess it means something whether we want to admit it or not."

He smiled. The corners of his eyes crinkled. "That's what I thought, too. I wanted to deny it, but there's no denying this."

"Okay, but we go slow," I said.

He nodded. "As long as we're both ready to admit it's something, we can go as slow as snails."

I laughed. "Sounds about perfect."

He took my hand and led me down the trail. "You want a pumpkin spice slush?"

I squinted at him. "Is that good?"

Axel placed a mocking hand on his heart. "You haven't lived until you've had a pumpkin spice slush. I don't even like pumpkin, but I get

161

one on the last night of the festival."

I tipped my face toward him. "Okay."

He smiled at me and I melted a little. "It might take a while. Why don't I meet you over by those buildings?"

"Okay. Sounds good."

I strode over between a couple of buildings and stood admiring the festivities. A few fireworks cracked in the sky and I watching, beaming at the display of beauty.

"Beautiful night, isn't it?"

I glanced over to see Mayor Potion strolling toward me.

"Sure is."

He jingled change in his pockets. "It seems they brought that boy in for questioning—the chicken farmer. That new police chief we've got seems to think he might've had something to do with Melbalean's murder."

"It seems like it," I said.

"I tell you, it's a weight off my mind. I'm glad the whole thing's about over. I hate to think that Magnolia Cove has a murderer running loose." He shot me a sad smile. "One who's slashing and dashing, as they say."

"That's true."

He rubbed his face. "But I tell you, a lot of folks are asking what happened to those golden eggs Melbalean had. The police have her chicken, have been keeping it quarantined, but they can't find those eggs."

I clutched my chest. "Oh. Well, I might know where they are."

The mayor smiled at me. "You do? Well, that would certainly help the police out a lot of they had 'em."

"Yes. In fact, we're standing on them."

"Well, I'll be," he said.

I found the mound that Betty had ditched the eggs under. I grabbed a nearby stick and peeled back the earth until the top of the bag was exposed.

"Here," he said, "let me help you with that."

"I've got it," I said.

He grabbed the bag at the same time as I did. The contents spilled onto the grass. There were half a dozen golden eggs and something else.

I gasped.

The other was a regular looking egg. It hit a rock and cracked open. The contents flowed out, and it's what was in there that made my heart stutter.

It was an image of the mayor looking upright and regal. I instantly knew what was going on. He had sold something to Melbalean, and in exchange, she'd trapped him.

I glanced up.

"I really wish you hadn't broken that egg," he said.

Mayor Potion held a gun to me.

"It was an accident," I said in a quiet voice. "And why are you using a gun when you're a wizard?"

"I like to keep things simple."

I smirked. "It was you."

"Come on out of the light, darlin', and we'll discuss it."

The last thing I wanted to do was lose sight of the party, but with a weapon leveled on me, I didn't think I had another option. I stepped away from the festival and from safety.

"You see I wasn't always a drunk," Potion said. "I used to be an upstanding citizen. But then my wife got very sick."

I eyed the gun and the steady hand that held it. I had to think, had to try to use my magic to get out of this. Maybe keeping him talking would work. "I'm sorry she got sick."

Wow. Brilliant. Tell the guy who's threatening to kill you that you're sorry his wife got sick. Smart.

"Well, so was I. I went to Melbalean. Asked if she could help. She could help all right, but I had to give her something. She wanted my reputation, basically—the thing I cherished most. As I said, I didn't always imbibe the way I do now."

I backed up. "Until Melbalean came along."

"That was the price I paid to get a few more years with my Susie. But then Susie passed on and I wanted my life back. Melbalean agreed. Said she'd give me the egg and I could become who I was again."

Thoughts swirled in my head. "But that wasn't enough, was it?"

He shook his head. "No. I wanted her to pay for taking things that folks gave her. She took what was dearest to you and seemed to have a sick glee for owning it. I knew it was crazy, but I'd read about an attack turkey somewhere. I planted the idea in Betty's head about a hen for this year's festival. Once she took the bait, I knew Melbalean would, too. I've got lots of friends, Pepper. Lots of friends. I had your grandmother's and Melbalean's birds circumvented to the post office in Hollyhock so I could see if the special feed I'd made worked, then I sent the birds on to the women."

"But why Betty's bird?" I said.

"Just in case the first bird didn't make it. See, I also had to control the hens. I had to make sure Melbalean's bird wouldn't remember killing her, and it took some work to make sure the creature would throw the blame on someone else."

"But what about Betty's? That bird didn't talk at all."

"Might not be smart enough. Chickens aren't particularly bright. But the feed worked. Made them mad."

I nodded in realization. "Then you planted some with Leona to throw suspicion on her and you planned to meet with Lane to throw suspicion on him. But instead of meeting Lane, you stole his feed— feed that looked exactly like what you had created. "

The mayor shrugged. "Anyone but me, darlin'. Anyone but me. The best part was that I used the cues of the fire to get Melbalean's bird to attack her, with the help of the food that made them aggressive, of course. The bird committed murder beautifully. Killed Melbalean just the way I wanted. But I still need my egg," he said, his face twisting harshly. "Otherwise, I'll never be who I once was."

Long dark shadows covered us. A sliver of moonlight glinted through the trees, reflecting off the gun.

"But now you know what happened, and I can't have that. So it looks like it's the end of the road for you, Pepper. Too bad. I hear you're mighty good at matching witches with their familiars."

He raised the gun to the level of my heart. Sweat drenched my skin and I knew this was it.

Use my magic or die.

Just then, a commotion came from behind us. Mint and Licky bumbled up. "It's dark back here," Mint said. "What are y'all doing?"

Never in my life was I so glad to see my aunts. 'Course, I could regret that feeling eventually, too.

The mayor turned, keeping the gun on me. "Just having a chat."

Licky reached Mayor Potion and put a hand on his shoulder. She peered over and yelled, "He's got a gun!"

Mint threw up her hands and screamed.

The gun flew from the mayor's hands into the air. A second later, it exploded into a thousand pieces.

Mint and Licky ran. I bolted past the mayor, who grabbed a handful of my hair. "Not so fast, little girl."

I yelled and my aunts stopped. They whirled around.

Mint took a step forward. "You release our niece right now."

The mayor's breath was hot in my ear. "I don't want to hurt more than one of you. But if I don't have a choice, I will."

Licky folded her arms and sank onto one hip. "You want to mess with chaos witches, go ahead. Be our guest."

I could see the mayor throw out his hand. At the same time, my aunts thrust their arms forward. Sparks rained on us. The mayor loosened his grip and I stumbled from his grasp. When I turned around, Mayor Potion stood surrounded by a tornado of magic.

I clutched for Mint, who pulled me into a hug.

The mayor screamed and spat. "Get me out of here. I'm the mayor of Magnolia Cove and I demand you release me."

Licky glanced at me. "You okay?"

"Yeah." I stared at the mayor. "He had Melbalean killed."

Mint released me. "I always knew there was something funny about him."

I watched as the magic tightened around him. "Do you know how to get him out of there?"

Licky laughed. "Of course not. We only know how to start chaos. Not how to stop it."

I laughed as the townsfolk started drifting into the patch of grass we were standing in. Mint turned to the crowd and said, "The mayor's a killer. Let's arrest him and go back to the party."

I laughed. Sounded like a plan to me.

TWENTY-THREE

*T*he sun was shining the next morning when I walked to Familiar Place. After Mint and Licky had wrapped up the mayor, Axel appeared with my pumpkin spice slush, which had been amazing, if I do say so myself. I explained what had happened and he called Garrick, who arrested Peter Potion.

Betty had listened quietly when I explained about the mayor. I think she felt duped by him. I mean, after all, she'd been waking up every morning at 4 am to save his rear end. I'd be a little ticked, too, if I discovered I was helping out a murderer.

But in the end, she didn't say anything. She just accepted it and went on.

What else could she do?

And the chickens? They were returned to where they came from—shipped overnight.

I sipped my tumbler of sweet tea with a few extra jellybeans thrown in as I padded down Bubbling Cauldron Road.

I snapped my fingers as I remembered there was one last thing I needed to do. I stopped by the statue of Amaryllis Snitch. Leona Doodle sat on a bench beside her. I plopped next to her and opened my purse.

I pulled out the bottle with the image of the beautiful woman from the egg and the cameo I'd found by the statue. "I assume this is yours," I said.

Leona's deep frown vanished when she saw what I held. "How did you know?"

I shrugged. "I didn't until I found the picture. You dropped it, right? And had been looking for it?"

She nodded slowly as she raised the bottle, tipping it left and right to admire the contents. "I never thought I'd see it again."

I smiled warmly. "I noticed the resemblance late last night and realized it was yours. I'm glad I could give this to you before you left."

She hugged the bottle to her chest. "I wanted to cook. Be the best cook in all of Alabama. I got my wish at a price. Thank you for this."

I patted her shoulder and said, "I'm glad I could help."

When Leona looked at me, tears misted her eyes. "You're welcome at my restaurant anytime you want. Anytime."

I thanked her and headed toward Familiar Place. My heart swelled with pride at the good deed I'd been able to do.

Other storeowners milled about the sidewalk, sweeping away the dirt. I waved to my neighbors and smiled.

I found a square box on the stoop. I wedged it under my arm and unlocked the door.

The animals yawned to life. The kittens stretched. The puppies yelped. I fed and watered them. I even let the puppies run across the floor to exercise.

The bell above the door tinkled.

"Morning," came the husky voice.

I glanced up from cleaning the glass counter. I wiped my hands and brushed a strand of crimson and honey hair from my face. "Morning."

Axel looked delicious in a navy blue t-shirt and hip-hugging jeans. He strolled up and leaned on the counter, being careful not to leave prints on the glass. "How're you feeling today?"

I shrugged. "Okay. It's crazy about the mayor, but what can we do?

I'm just glad I didn't get shot. I have my aunts to thank for that. For once, their chaos magic did the right thing."

His blue eyes shone when he smiled. My heart fluttered and I felt heat creep up my neck. "I just came by to make sure you're okay and see if you wanted to have some lunch."

I laughed. "The way our dates go, someone will wind up dead."

He shook his head. "Not at lunch. Supper, maybe."

I smiled. "You've got a point. Okay, let's have some lunch. I should be able to close up shop for an hour."

Axel's gaze trailed to the box. "What's that?"

I shook my head. "No idea. It was on my doorstep when I arrived. I haven't had a chance to look at it."

I grabbed a pair of scissors and sliced open the top. I pulled away a nest of packing straw until I found what looked like a set of instructions. I handed them to Axel as I pulled out the contents.

It was a plum-colored egg, about eight inches high and quite round. It came with a base, which I set it on.

"Oh. Is this some sort of gift? Something I'm supposed to put up somewhere and display?" I said.

Axel didn't answer. I kept digging until I found a package slip. The receiver was supposed to have been my Uncle Donovan.

"Uncle Donovan must've ordered this before he died," I murmured, picking it up and admiring the jeweled color. "What is it?"

Axel glanced up from the instruction sheet. "Are you ready for this?"

I shrugged. "Sure. What is it?"

He glanced from the egg to me. "It's a dragon's egg."

I nearly dropped it on the counter. I set it in its holder. "What? It's a what?"

"A dragon egg."

A bolt of fear shot down my spine. "Dragons don't exist. I sell puppies and kittens and birds. I do not sell dragons. I do not, I repeat, sell dragons. They breathe fire and hurt things—like people. At least that's what happens in all the fairy tales and myths."

Axel smiled coyly. "I'm afraid to tell you that I think you're supposed to do now."

The egg jiggled as it sat in the cradle. A small crack appeared on top. I threw Axel a terrified look. "What's it doing?"

Axel crossed to me and placed a hand on my shoulder. "Hatching."

Oh, boy.

<<<<>>>>

THANK Y'ALL!

Pepper's adventures continue in Southern Myths, the next book in the
Sweet Tea Witch Mysteries Series.
Click HERE to order.

Thank you so much for reading SOUTHERN SPELLS. If you enjoyed it, please consider leaving a review. Reviews help other readers decide whether they'd like to take a chance on a book. If you think they should take a chance on this one, let them know!

CLICK HERE to leave a review.

And I love to hear from you! Please feel free to drop me a line anytime. You can email me amy@amyboylesauthor.com.

ALSO BY AMY BOYLES

SWEET TEA WICH MYSTERIES
SOUTHERN MAGIC
SOUTHERN SPELLS
SOUTHERN MYTHS

BLESS YOUR WITCH SERIES
SCARED WITCHLESS
KISS MY WITCH
QUEEN WITCH
QUIT YOUR WITCHIN'
FOR WITCH'S SAKE
DON'T GIVE A WITCH
WITCH MY GRITS
FRIED GREEN WITCH
SOUTHERN WITCHING

SOUTHERN SINGLE MOM PARANORMAL MYSTERIES
The Witch's Handbook to Hunting Vampires
The Witch's Handbook to Catching Werewolves
The Witch's Handbook to Trapping Demons

ABOUT THE AUTHOR

Amy Boyles grew up reading Judy Blume and Christopher Pike. Somehow, the combination of coming of age books and teenage murder mysteries made her want to be a writer. After graduating college at DePauw University, she spent some time living in Chicago, Louisville, and New York before settling back in the South. Now, she spends her time chasing two preschoolers while trying to stir up trouble in Silver Springs, Alabama, the fictional town where Dylan Apel and her sisters are trying to master witchcraft, tame their crazy relatives, and juggle their love lives. She loves to hear from readers! You can email her at amy@amyboylesauthor.com.

CPSIA information can be obtained
at www.ICGtesting.com
Printed in the USA
LVHW100829250223
740414LV00016B/100